NEW HORIZONS

A collection of short stories and poems

by LiterEight
a group of eight Scottish-based female writers

ACKNOWLEDGEMENTS

The authors would like to thank Ronald Lang for the photograph used on the cover and John Atchison for the cover design and for his continuing support with the LiterEight website.

Cover Image: Sunset over Ailsa Craig, Firth of Clyde
© RFS Lang 2011

New Horizons

A selection of stories and poems in various genres

New Horizons
by Catherine Lang

Andrew Boyd hunched over his computer, engrossed in the image of a pale man handing a platinum box to the US President. A giant telescope in the bay window behind his desk peered blindly into the night while the study walls bore witness to a lifetime spent looking beyond the atmosphere. Only a painting of a young family showed a more down-to-earth devotion.

Suddenly a dark haired girl rushed in. Andrew scowled. "Paula, I'm not to be disturbed. I need to reread the President's statement."

"Sorry, Gramps, but there's someone here who insists on seeing you immediately."

Paula stepped aside to reveal a tall, gaunt man whose elegant dark glasses served to accentuate his sallow skin and blonde hair.

Turning almost as ashen as his guest, Andrew leapt to his feet.

"Kerebos!"

"Hello, Andrew," said a melodic voice.

"I never thought to see you again," stammered Andrew. "Come, sit down." He glanced at his granddaughter who reluctantly left the room.

"Kerebos, why on earth are you here?"

Settling himself, Kerebos responded, "Very well phrased. Why, on Earth, indeed? I too thought that when we parted in 1972 after Apollo we would never meet again. Time has not been kind to you."

"At 65 I find that younger minds are making the discoveries, though I do try to stay informed. As

---

for my family..." Andrew sighed, staring at the painting. "My son, Paul, his wife and mine all died in that pointless New York attack. Only Paula was spared to me. She was ill so stayed behind. From the safety of this study, filled with dreams of moons and stars, we watched the stability we took for granted crumble with the Towers."

"A beautiful young woman, and gifted," commented Kerebos.

Andrew glanced quickly at his visitor's face and then away. "She is studying astrophysics. Even at 20 her insights surpass mine and her father's. Paula kept me sane. Her presence, and the knowledge that old friends from across the political spectrum were all striving for harmony rather than conflict. But what can you want with her or with me now?"

Kerebos made no reply

"You have come with these emissaries?" asked Andrew. "As soon as I saw the President's announcement yesterday I recognised the man who had given him the strange gift. By his looks, I guessed where he had come from."

"You must have known that the reviving interest in travel to the stars could rekindle our involvement. The Quora were prepared to accept your ventures to the Moon, the Mars Explorer and even journeys as far as the gas giants, but again Pluto has come within your scientists' sights. New Horizons has been launched and in a very few of your years the last outpost of the Quora's civilization could come into your sphere of influence."

Andrew groaned and sank into a chair. "I hoped that when they downgraded Pluto's planet status they would leave it unexplored. When you

—

told me forty years ago how important it was to the Quora I foolishly thought it too far away to be of any interest. Is there still time to avert disaster?"

"It would be easiest for me to show you," said Kerebos.

Removing his glasses, Kerebos stared at Andrew who avoided making contact with the vibrant yellow eyes.

"Come, Andrew. It wouldn't be the first time you'd travelled in my mind."

"Your powers unnerve me."

"As they should. But they are miniscule in comparison to those of the Quora when they are united. The time of trial is here and it will affect the whole human race."

"What trial? I thought your masters had a rule about not interfering with lesser species, letting them develop and learn for themselves."

"Up to a point – and that point is the survival of their realm, of the Universe beyond."

Andrew shrugged, "How can an unmanned probe, which will take years to travel to the far end of the solar system, impact on a race as advanced as your creator's?"

"Even powerful beings have a weakness. Pluto is theirs," admitted Kerebos. "It is almost eighty Earth years since one of your kind realised it existed. For the Quora time passes much more slowly. They live one year for every orbit of the Sun so that they and we who serve them age almost infinitesimally in comparison to you.

"To them scarcely 100 days have passed since that first discovery and now they sense that, in too short a time for them to do anything further to protect themselves, Pluto will be probed and photographed. New Horizons will fly close enough to recognise that the ring of tiny moons is not a natural formation. Your scientists will want to investigate further, to make landfall."

"But it would take years to create the necessary equipment and even more to raise the funds," declared Andrew.

"The Quora cannot take the risk, so they have sent the emissaries to meet the world's leaders."

Andrew moved uneasily in his chair.

"Where is the danger in five men each visiting one of the five continents, bearing a gift? What point is there in this contact?"

Kerebos sighed, "When life was seeded throughout the Galaxy, it was agreed that the individual life-forms which developed would own their planets where they could learn to work together. When they reached a proper level of unity and harmony they could be invited to move to the next level. It was believed – many worlds have proved it true – that if they focused on discord and competition, by the time they achieved the technology to spread that disharmony beyond their own atmospheres, they would destroy themselves. Earth has come close, yet you managed to end the Cold War. Old enemies started to work together above the Earth, if not always on it. Then came a more insidious enmity.

"Like Nine Eleven," asked Andrew, staring at the painting. "So many people died, so many lives ripped apart, then and since, and for what?"

"For dogma, for a passionate belief that only one way is the right way, for overall power," declared Kerebos unemotionally. "These warriors are prepared to die for their cause, however outrageous, and to destroy myriad others in the process."

"So our self-destruction is assured," sighed Andrew.

"Perhaps. One faction is focused on moulding the world into their ideal form, no matter the cost, while others have set their sights on venturing further out into the cosmos," continued Kerebos.

"But still I don't understand," said Andrew. "What can we possibly do that would affect the Quora?"

"Your concept of time is so very different from theirs. The moon, the other planets exist within your perception of time. As soon as anything from Earth touches the moons of Pluto it too will be pulled into your time. The Quora have lived for almost eternity but increasingly they have found access to this realm diminishing. Pluto is the final gateway. Lose that last portal and they must relinquish their influence here. That they are unwilling to do."

Andrew sighed. "So the Quora police our Universe but cannot exist within it?"

Kerebos nodded. "In a way. Their role is to bring certain races under their wing and to ensure that others do not disturb the delicate balance of the true Universe beyond. They must ensure that Pluto is not contaminated."

"So these envoys are merely a diversion?" asked Andrew

"No, we have gone beyond that. They created us to work with those who, like you, realised that it is not too little knowledge that is dangerous, but too much. We seemed to have succeeded in slowing

11

down the push to the stars, but it is clear that questing minds cannot be held back."

"I was one of those minds, once, as Paula is now. Astrophysics in the 60s and afterwards has done much to benefit humankind. We have to continue."

Kerebos sighed and shook his head.

"So what happens now?" asked Andrew.

"Your scientists have many differing ideas about your Universe," said Kerebos. "A few, like you, have seen beyond the physical boundaries, yet it would be impossible to conceive of the reality. As I have said, most planets self-destruct before they reach beyond their own atmosphere."

Andrew regarded Kerebos very seriously, but still avoiding those absorbing eyes. "Are you trying to tell me that this destruction is no accident – that these worlds are helped to their own annihilation?"

"No, no ... never that!" exclaimed Kerebos. "Not every planet has failed the test. But with Earth we have had to come earlier than we would have hoped – before enough minds like yours are open to the opportunities."

Andrew looked aghast. "So, these men are part of the trial?"

"Yes. When you started striving to break through the atmosphere, when you and men like you began to create the machinery to reach beyond your planet, your own little Moon, the Quora put in place this plan. Remember, for them it was only a short time ago. Part of my role when I visited here when you were a young man was an assessment of what would need to be done if our original strategy failed."

"Kerebos, I thought you were my friend."

"I am, Andrew, but I must serve a greater good. This trial can be passed but it requires all the world's nations to work together. What your leaders are being offered individually by each of the envoys is part of a tool to physical and spiritual advancement. But it can only be achieved in peace and unity.

"The five segments are each apparently alike, but only when they come together will they provide the instrument that can move your race into the next realm. Use any of them individually and destruction is inevitable. Who has the power to convince the leaders of these lands to join together, to trust each other, to work for the benefit of everyone? Our envoys will try but will they be believed. Do you, who achieved so much, know a way to achieve consensus?"

Andrew put his head in his hands.

"I doubt I have that influence. Younger minds have taken over and we who started the march to the stars are left to our telescopes and our dreams."

"Then Earth is doomed. It may take another twenty-five years but without unity, progression is impossible."

Andrew suddenly reddened.

"So why did you come? Why risk exposing yourself to our time just to tell me that?"

"I came to offer you a chance."

"Yes, chance for my world."

"No, a chance for you."

"What?"

"To return with me."

"But I am of the Earth. How can I come with you and not cause the very destruction you have described?" asked Andrew.

Kerebos smiled. "The gift I gave you long ago will protect us. You can grow old slowly and see the Galaxy from our perspective, full of life and opportunity."

"But I cannot watch my world destroy itself, without trying to help."

"That has to be your decision. I will not be permitted to return and you cannot come unaided."

As his guest sat unmoving, Andrew rose and paced the room. "I may not live twenty-five years, yet I cannot walk away. But there is someone that you can take in my place."

Paula entered quietly. "You called for me, grandfather?"

Kerebos looked at Andrew who smiled, meeting the stranger's eyes for the first time.

"I passed your gift to my granddaughter the day her father died. She walks in my mind and I in hers. Paula, this is Kerebos whom I told you about that day. Go with him."

"But Gramps, I want to stay and help you," cried the girl.

"Paula, you are all I have. If you go with him, you will have eternity and I can try to turn this tide. If I succeed we will meet again soon."

Nodding to Andrew, Kerebos rose and turned his penetrating gaze on Paula.

"Look deep into his eyes," said her grandfather, turning to gaze at the stars.

—

The Charge of the Sunflowers

by Greta Yorke

New recruits in verdant camouflage
dig in
hug soil.
Initial training sees them stretch,
achieve status in the ranks.
Colours gained, regimental heads unfold
revealing Fibonacci faces,
each one citron fringed and epauletted green.
Uniform legionnaires sway
in breeze rippling rows,
drilled troopers stand fast against mightier forces.
Throughout the tour they hold ground
protecting, nurturing their commission,
basking as nectar is drawn.
Duty done, lustre leeched,
jaundiced scalps surrender
mark time
await the fall.
Bedraggled ochre frills frame faces withered,
black pellet charges exposed in rigid pits.
Decommissioned,
condemned,
no court martial, no repeal.
Silence explodes.
Rhythmic
reaper
takes
its
toll.

A Special Place
by Fiona Atchison

The view is a spectacular sandwich of yellowed rock speckled with conifers set between the blues of sky and sea. The room is spacious, the balcony newly re-tiled and walls painted in pale grey. I don't miss the previous glaring white. Visiting Majorca and this hotel for the past twelve years with my wife Doreen is a habit that's become hard to break. Some would say tedious, I suppose. For instance, I know shirts, shorts, trousers and shoes will be stored away in the wardrobe with those earmarked for day and evening. I know that over the next fourteen days we alternate every two nights between the two hotel restaurants. A bottle of red wine one night and white the next. We alternate those same restaurants every day for breakfast and eat a 'full English' instead of cereal.

As this is the first evening of arrival I find the regular staff smile warmly in recognition. One in particular, the restaurant manager of the *Olivo*, falters slightly then is most profuse in his welcome. We shake hands like old friends. He strides to a table, making much of us as we sit. I feel gratified. A few changes catch my eye; a new coffee machine has replaced the waiter's jug. The wine list is more expensive, yet I still order Champagne for the first night.

The conversation skims over platitudes, the food and what we will do tomorrow. This latter topic I know by rote. On the morning of our first day we will breakfast early. At nine-thirty, I will secure sun loungers close to the bar and small pool, but essentially for the shade and proximity of toilets. At eleven I will go to the open air bar and order two white coffees, "dos café con leche por favor", and we will savour them slowly. At lunch we will walk along the single strand of shops and cafés pretending to decide, yet gravitating to *Celesta's* on the corner. A shared pizza with two small beers and we will people-watch for an hour or so. Then reading, a touch of sunbathing and a short cold swim will drain the remains of the afternoon. We will lie on our beds for a while, mustering the energy for shower and change. Hair will be washed and styled, dress and jewellery assembled and make up adhered. I will drop into shirt and trousers and pour a glass of chilled Cava from the small fridge. I will take a photograph using the camera's timer. Another for the album, only the hair greying and stomach extending to tell the years apart.

Later, we will eat another four course meal and see whatever entertainment the hotel programme has on offer for the evening. As the week goes by we might forsake the live music and dancing for long moonlit walks along the horseshoe sands and return for a nightcap. As I glimpse the days ahead, a sudden mundaneness, a feeling of futility catches my throat. This place no longer holds any magic for me. I feel lost as I reach over and take your hand. I realise too late, coming here again with you has been a mistake. For you are not Doreen and, although the place and the rituals are the same, I just want to go home. You pat my hand. In those soft brown eyes, I see you understand.

And of course you do, my darling daughter, for you miss your mother as much as I miss my wife.

I see me

by Fiona McFadzean

Back then
I see her in her ballet dress,
toe pointed, arms aloft,
frown of concentration,
trying her best to get it right
and I see me.

I see her in the netball team,
running, turning, arms outstretched,
grabbing the ball,
trying her best to find the net
and I see me.

I see her in the junior choir
hands clasped, eye on conductor
lips a perfect Oh,
trying her best to reach top note
and I see me.

And now
I see her in her graduation gown,
hand held scroll, an Honours Degree,
with beaming smile
fearlessly facing an unknown future
and I see her dad.

I wonder if he managed to scale his Everests
unaware of the mountain he left for me
to climb alone.
My daughter looks my way, blows a kiss,
We mouth "Love you." Mime high five,
And I see me again.

The Love of My Life

by Helena Sheridan

"Everyone, this is Lorel." Jack nervously presented the latest woman in his life.

He drew an affectionate hand down her flawless cheek. Lorel's expression remained serene. He envied her cool composure. This was the moment he had dreaded for ages. How would his critical friends react? She was so unlike any of the others he had introduced to them – would they approve of her?

His heart thumped in expectation at the buzz of excitable chatter. Gradually, a ripple of congratulatory approval welled from the back of the room. Jack closed his eyes with relief and turned to Lorel, but a swirl of eager guests surrounded her, thoughtlessly pushing him from her side.

Gripped by wild possessiveness, he tried to nudge his way forward again. If he could just touch her – but caught by a second flow of well-wishers he found himself drifting further away.

Reluctantly, he conceded to the crowd's enthusiasm. It was hardly unexpected. Lorel was beautiful and definitely the best thing that had ever happened to him for a long time. From the moment she entered his life he knew things would never be the same again!

"Lorel! Lorel!" Her sweet, angelic name pounded like a mystic chant in his mind. "Lore lei?" he mused. A wry smile creased his tired face as he gazed across the room at her.

With the evening going well, Jack slipped back from the throng. Totally intoxicated by a mixture of heady emotions and a large brandy, he surveyed the jubilant party, mentally indexing those present.

Michael, Jane, Fred ... Amelia?

"Amelia! How the hell?" His knuckles whitened around his empty glass as he considered his ex-partner.

Amelia glared back, tossing her blonde ponytail in pure defiance. She had not taken kindly to rejection and his overwhelming devotion to the new woman in his life. Jack felt his stomach lurch with uncertainty. Amelia's behaviour was always unpredictable. Her unwelcome presence at the function could only mean trouble.

He could just see Lorel's head amongst the crowd. For the moment she was safe from any fevered outbursts. He noted the jealous glint in Amelia's hazel eyes as she snaked menacingly towards her rival. He had to remove her from the room before she embroiled him in another ugly scene.

"What do you think you're doing here?" Jack pounced, swerving her from her decided course.

Amelia reeled back. Shaking her arm free of his steely grasp, she lolled seductively against the wall.

"Thought I'd come along and see what all the fuss was about. I'm simply interested to see what she's like. So, that's *her?*" She gestured disapprovingly.

Jack remained silent, his attention fixed on the hostile gate-crasher. He longed to steer Amelia to the door and get her out as quickly as possible, but the thought of the inevitable uproar made him cringe.

When challenged, she thought nothing of striking out with little regard for those she hurt.

"Look, I don't want any trouble," he cautioned. Amelia basked in his unease. Blowing a taunting kiss she claimed occupancy of a nearby chair.

The light-hearted crowd continued to jostle about them. "How did you do it, pal? Lorel's absolutely gorgeous," one complimented, slapping Jack firmly on the back.

Amelia writhed at the tribute. "Perhaps I should tell them what I think of her, eh Jack?" she baited.

His flushed face made Amelia snigger. He had witnessed several of her dark moods in the past enough times to know she was harbouring another.

"Get out!" Jack ordered, trying to muffle his angry tone just in case anyone else heard the exchange.

"I'm not leaving," she announced. "I was here first, remember?"

Jack shook his head at the ironic truth. Amelia was right, but strangely had only herself to blame for losing him. She knew how to lift his spirits from those dreadful times of deep depression. Her zany, outrageous antics had made him laugh and helped him through the bleak uninspired winter. With his hopes renewed it was inevitable things would change … only they didn't change in the way she would have liked.

Suddenly there was Lorel, like a rush of fresh spring air. She occupied each waking hour and filled his dreams. He could not deny her. Lorel was what he had been waiting for all his life…

—

He glanced back at the chattering company. Still hedged by admirers, Lorel stood elegantly at the far end of the room.

"Oh come on, Amelia give me a break, why don't you?" Jack tried to reason.

Amelia stiffened her shoulders. Her eyes sparked with sinister amusement.

"Sure, if that's what you want, Jack, I'll give you a break!"

Her attractive face contorted with smouldering revenge as she sprang from the chair and ventured towards the crowd.

Jack wrenched at her arm but with an ungainly shove she catapulted him aside and continued to march towards Lorel.

"No, Amelia! Please, no!" Jack begged, but she was determined to regain centre stage.

Her loud ranting sent a murmur of disapproval amongst the embarrassed onlookers. Crazed with jealousy, Amelia leapt at her adversary. Shrieks of horror and outrage accompanied the confrontation. Shaking from Amelia's savage blows, Lorel fell back, hitting her head on the edge of a heavy table. The resultant crash echoed in the high vaulted ceiling. Jack raced to intervene, but it was too late.

Lorel lay sprawled across the wooden floor. He bent at her side, but there was nothing he could do. Amelia staggered away cringing against the crowd's fierce objections. Like a distressed child, Jack wrapped his arms about his knees and rocked from side to side.

The past few months spent with Lorel had been the happiest he had ever known. He should have realised Amelia would not give up. With unwavering determination she had fought hard to win back his affection. Her arms outstretched, she appealed to him for support, but he turned away in disgust. How could he ever forgive her for shattering his dream?

Paled and silent, he stared in horror at Lorel's cold, disfigured face. Their future together had been assured – now it was over.

Although completely different from his usual style, his artistic friends agreed Lorel was the best statue the sculptor had ever created.

Ode to a Cold Caller

by Lesley Deschner

I don't need double glazing,
the Council put it in.
My kitchen won't need fitted
since I only cook for one.
My bedrooms are just fine as well,
they have all that they need.
My bathroom doesn't need replaced,
I'm sure it has no leaks.
My pipes have all been lagged quite well;
my loft is insulated.
My water has no lead at all,
and my heating's integrated.
My finances are my own biz, dear,
now don't you think it's rude,
to ask such searching questions?
Do you really think you should?
Look, I know you have a job to do,
I really understand,
but please consider my free time,
I don't have much to hand.
Now, if I had the cash to spend,
and wanted so to do,
I'd plan the changes carefully,
and then I'd call on YOU!

Walking on Parapets

by Janice Johnston

Some tendril of memory made me slam on the brakes. The car slewed into the verge and stopped.

I forced myself to look left, through the branches of the trees, and search for the soft red stone of the house.

We used to live here, you see. In the house in the lee of the hill. The one with bay windows surrounded by ivy and looking out to amazing views over the valley.

A picture-perfect house for a picture-perfect family.

I shook my head. It must be eight, no, probably closer to ten years since we left. What made me come this way to town?

Belatedly, I glanced in the mirror. The road behind was clear. I stared at the clock, knowing – before I calculated how much time I would need to reach the town centre, park and find the right building – that I would walk down to the stream.

I abandoned the car at the roadside and crossed over to the side road. The tarmac was rough with a ribbon of grass trailing down the centre, the wooden gate in the hedgerow still balanced on a single hinge. How many times had I walked this way, I wondered – five times a week, say, for eleven, twelve years?

Maths was never my strong point but the walk had certainly imprinted itself in my mind. Instinctively, I stepped past the space where a long dead bush had always caught my clothing.

This time no children demanded my attention, no dog bounded along bumping into me. I had time to relax and calm myself before my job interview in town.

Pinkish purple swords of Rosebay Willowherb towered above white Clover and Ragged Robin in the deep verge. I smiled at how the names came back to me. Chloe always had to know the proper names. We would carefully carry a small sample back home and pore over a wildflower book till we found the matching picture.

Ryan was always too busy tearing along to think about nature. He must have covered the distance five times over for each walk, on every possible wheeled toy; tricycles to mountain bikes, scooters to skateboards. In their early years I hardly had time to admire the view, I was too busy watching for traffic or other dangers. The children never seemed to bother though. Perhaps I worried enough for all of us.

A sudden twist in the road brought me to the sandstone bridge over the stream. Weeds sprouted from damaged pointing, the soft stone was pitted with years of weathering, yet it still glowed in the sunshine.

There was a garish concrete repair in one corner. Childishly, I hoped that the speeding car had suffered more damage than the bridge.

This was a country lane, for God's sake, not the driver's own personal Silverstone. Some drivers, though, didn't seem to think of what might be round the corner.

In the still air I imagined I felt Willow nuzzling my hand, pushing herself against my legs.

The car that had hit her hadn't stopped.

It speeded off, leaving Ryan, Chloe and me to find Willow lying where she'd been flung, her big loving eyes glazed over, her boundless energy halted.

It was then that I realised for the first time I couldn't always protect my family, no matter how hard I tried.

We buried Willow in a corner of the garden and planted a tree, one Chloe found in her book, in her memory – the rust-coloured leaves the same shade as Willow's soft coat.

That was the beginning of the end of our picture-perfect life.

My almost daily walks to the bridge became a balm, an oasis of calm after a day filled with tension and arguments with John. We both knew our marriage was over but neither of us would admit it. The children, teenagers by that time, often found serenity by the stream, too. We would walk back discussing football matches or suitable lengths for school skirts, Chloe clutching yet another specimen to compare to the pictures in the now dog-eared wildflower book.

I leaned over the parapet, feeling the rough, gritty stonework under my hands and startled a pair of ducks. They clattered their wings against the water then, gaining height, flew out of sight. I jerked upright, heart pounding, throat grasping air, my mind tumbling backwards to another heart-pounding moment at the bridge.

Ryan, fourteen, maybe fifteen, telling me exactly how he'd scored the winning goal on Saturday, kick by kick. Casually, still talking, he jumped up on the parapet and walked along the flat surface. It was obvious from his easy confidence that this wasn't the first time. He had no fear.

My limbs turned to ice while my mind flashed pictures of him falling, breaking bones, drowning, dying.

"Get. Down. Now." I struggled to stay calm.

He looked puzzled then, seeing my face, he shrugged his shoulders and jumped down. He'd never anticipated any danger.

I sighed. Perhaps I had been overprotective of the children but that summer had been so awful, what with Willow being killed, then John walking out.

Chloe, Ryan and I had had to move into a small flat in town. I'd taken dead-end jobs, more for the suitability of the hours than for any job satisfaction. I hated that time, hated having to make all the decisions and worrying about everything.

I glanced at my watch, still time to spare. Chloe and Ryan are walking other parapets now, on their own, no neurotic mother hovering nearby. They're doing well, enjoying life. Perhaps it's time for me to follow their example. This interview is for a job that's a total departure for me, something I really want to do. It's no easy, make-do job to fit in with everyone else's needs.

Leaning over the parapet again I checked to see if the hawthorn is still there. That last spring, the creamy white flowers had blanketed the bush. I watched the stream meandering into the distance.

I remembered Ryan's fearlessness.

Slowly, I pulled myself up onto the parapet. The water was a good fifteen feet below. If I fell I would break bones, at the very least.

Taking a deep breath, I walked across the square-cut stones – not looking down – only ahead.

Regeneration

by Fiona McFadzean

For sixty five years
the Mill hooter's strident call bade weft and weavers
to their looms, tending to shuttle, bobbin and teazle,
producing fine cloth to suit a nation; the constant click
and clack killing conversation, communication only
through body language.

Until, without warning,
that rogue, Recession, reared his ugly head, bit hard,
chewed up, moved on, leaving a shocked workforce
of idle hands in eerie silence, conversing in whispers,
no hope for tomorrow.

Yet all was not lost.
Those worthies, Will and Way, stepped in, Autumn club
dominoes exchanged for Spring in step business plans;
with ancestral grit they passed their message on, rallied
children's children to their cause.

Today's tourists
flock to a living, working museum, learn the old ways
while trying the new; craft their own souvenirs, a cut
glass brooch, a wobbly pot, a brushed felt accessory.
Three generations pulling together.
Business as usual.

A Suitable Arrangement

by Maggie Bolton

The room was small but pleasantly appointed, quite appropriate for a wedding with so few guests. Apart from the bride and groom and the officiating officer, there was only a handful of friends and colleagues present. As for family – well there was just me; his father refused to come. There were flowers everywhere. I think they were actually real, though it's hard to tell these days. Their mingled, heady scents added another surreal quality to this extraordinary wedding. Mind you, perhaps it's not so extraordinary – perhaps we're just old-fashioned.

I watched my son gaze lovingly into the eyes of his diminutive but flawlessly beautiful bride and, I confess, I felt the tears well up. Who would have imagined our studious but socially inept son marrying such a stunner? I couldn't help but feel concerned though – it was all so sudden. *Marry in haste; repent at leisure* they used to say. I furtively dabbed my eyes as I tried to put on a happy face and quash my nagging doubts. After all, it's traditionally the mother of the *bride* rather than the groom who is supposed to weep at weddings, isn't it?

The bride was given away not by her father, but by the Managing Director of The Lunar Research and Trading Company for whom they both worked. I must say I have always found the expression *given away* rather distasteful, as if a bride was disposable property; a prize or a merchandising free gift perhaps. I suppose in past centuries this was indeed the case, and maybe... My musings were cut short as the ceremony finished and the room filled with music in a triumphal crescendo. The bride bestowed her enchanting smile equally on each guest in turn and then on her new husband. He gazed back, his delight and adoration so palpable it made my heart lurch. He was clearly besotted, but surely he could see that it was one-way traffic. Making their way through the group of congratulatory friends, they eventually came to me.

"Mum," Justin said, "Brilliant that you got here in time. Sorry it's all been a bit of a rush, but we *have* to leave tonight with all our equipment and, these days, seats on the Space-Station Shuttle are like rocking-horse shi ..."

"*Darling!*" interrupted the bride in pseudo-shocked admonishing tones.

It was subtly done – so apparently affectionate but so controlling. I gritted my teeth.

"Sorry Angel," my son said obediently, looking suitably chastened for what was, to my mind, the very minor crime of attempting to bring the word 'shit' into the conversation. Turning to me he added, "Mum, I'd like you to meet Liana ... my wife."

His proud yet bashful grin reminded me so much of the time when, as an eight-year-old, he had been presented with the school science prize. On that occasion his father and I had watched him with joy and pride. Now my emotions were so jangled I found it extremely hard to respond. Liana stepped forward.

"It's such a pleasure to meet you at last," she said, "I've heard so much about you, I feel I know you already ... mother. May I call you that?"

Such a trite little speech, I thought, and totally false. I was seething, yet unwilling to cause a scene for Justin's sake. It was then that she took my hand and, leaning forward, gave me a brief kiss on the cheek. I hope I didn't flinch, or if I did that she didn't detect it. Her touch was warm and gentle and her kiss as light as a butterfly. I suppose I must have muttered something suitable in reply – don't ask me what. Fortunately friends gathered round at that point so the awkward moment passed.

"Ha, it really will be a honey*moon*," said someone with an over-bright, self-conscious laugh, "quite a long one too. How long will you be marooned at that lunar outpost, Justin – three years is it? Rather you than me. But of course you'll have your delightful bride at your side..."

The appalling little man gave a coyly suggestive smirk which Justin chose to disregard – or more likely, just didn't see.

"Yes," he said, "three years, with the option to stay on for a while if the research programme takes longer than we expect and well, apart from the occasional trading convoys, it will be just the two of us."

Did I detect a flicker of uncertainty there? Had he only just realised the enormity of what he was about to undertake, and with a wife whom, no matter how deeply in love he might imagine himself to be, he really hardly knew? It was quite possible. For a highly intelligent man he could be extremely slow in some areas of understanding. But it was a done deal. There would be little point in rocking the boat now. I wished I could share my concerns with his father, but he had already made his opinion abundantly clear, insisting that, if Justin went through with it, he would never speak to him again. So perhaps it's just as well he wasn't here. I tried hard to hide my feelings, but clearly I wasn't doing a great job. I felt a light touch on my arm.

"Don't worry," Liana said quietly, "I'll take good care of him and make him happy. We've worked together on the project right from the start, so I can help him in his work as well as fulfilling his ... you know ... personal needs.'

"Hmm," I said vaguely.

There was one thing she *couldn't* do, I thought, but didn't like to mention it. It had been one of my first objections – Justin was, after all, our only child.

Perhaps I was being unfair. She was trying her best to be nice, but this was all too much. I'm not a great drinker, but I suddenly thought that alcohol might go some way towards stiffening up the sinews. Liana must have had the same idea.

"Here, would you like this?" she said, "Someone just handed it to me, but I don't drink."

"Thanks," I said, taking the offered brandy glass and downing its contents in one, un-ladylike gulp.

It certainly mellowed me and we sat in fairly companionable silence for a while until another thought occurred to me.

"What happens in the future when he gets old and wrinkled and cranky?" I said.

Liana shrugged, "Perhaps I shall get old and cranky too – who knows? Anyway, if things get too sticky there's always divorce. Really you know, this marriage is no more of a gamble than any other."

34

I searched her face, looking for falsehood and artifice. Maybe I wasn't seeing too clearly after that brandy, but her concerned look seemed real enough to me.

"Please be happy for us ... Mum," she said with a wistful smile, and left before I could respond.

I sat thinking for a long while. Poor Justin, he was so keen on his lunar research project that even when that skin-flint company told him the three-year funding could only be for one, it hadn't put him off – he would have gone out there alone if necessary. Personally I think they were hoping he'd give up the whole, ridiculously expensive project. When he was still determined to go, rather than have him go stir-crazy all by himself and wreck the place, they came up with a plan. They must have suspected Justin's feelings for Liana and put her up to it, as he certainly would never have made the first move. No, he would have simply hugged his guilty longings to himself and worshipped her from afar. Shy and awkward, Justin had never had much success with girls, yet here he was, looking so happy with his beautiful new wife. Surely I should be pleased for him.

I sighed. Under the circumstances, apart of course from the fact that there would be no grandchildren for us, perhaps Justin's marriage to an artificial humanoid was really the only sensible option.

Spring
by Greta Yorke

Darkness contained within your warmth,
sharpness softens,
as pendulous prophets herald your arrival
in virgin silence.
Deep forces explode from papery tunics
splotching crisp hues
on nature's palette
while twitterings,
punctuated by guttural guiros,
confirm migrants' return.

Sea Glass
by Greta Yorke

Sand to sand
fragments, deposited by reluctant retreat
pepper the shoreline.
Exposed by sun,
translucence turned opaque
spearmint smooth.
Recrafted remnants of Buckie or Chanel
danger shards eroded by saline tumble,
littoral trove.

A Gift of Love

by Catherine Lang

Theo stared solemnly out of the cottage window, drinking in the scene. The immaculate lawn was strewn with russet leaves, the height and girth of the gnarled chestnut underlining the passage of time. He had often sat in its shade with Susan and her grandmother but today might be the last time he would enjoy its beauty.

Theo took a long, hard look at his reflection in the glass. He had to admit that his hair was thinning, just like the leaves. The reddish brown crop was not as luxuriant as it had once been, but there wasn't a trace of grey. And, apart from the incipient baldness, the face showed little trace of age, the eyes shining with the same lustre they had always had.

His reverie was interrupted by the sound of a woman singing in the passageway. She breezed into the room, deftly avoiding the huge pile of boxes. Theo waited expectantly but she only paused briefly to kiss him on the forehead as she moved across the room.

"Beautiful morning, old thing!"

"A bit less of the old, if you please," he silently growled, but she ignored him as she dumped the pile of mail on the chair in the window and disappeared out again, still humming. He never could identify what she sang, but it was good to hear her enjoying her music.

It was under the chestnut tree that they had first met, four decades ago, and he felt he knew her better than anyone. As they had grown closer, he had spent

—

many hours sitting just listening to her pour out her heart to him – the loss of her parents, her passion for music and her longing for someone to love. He had been her only confidante and he was proud of what he had helped her become. There had been a few false starts and many tears before she had finally found Mr Right, and he'd been there to lend a shoulder to cry on throughout. Theo had been delighted when she told him – before anyone else even suspected – that she'd finally met the man of her dreams.

When Susan married Peter and moved into her grandmother's country cottage, Theo had expected to be progressively left behind, but to his delight their friendship had continued through the years. He had watched her find success as a musician and happiness as a wife. There had been a few tears, when she learned that there would be no children, and a lot of joy – and he had shared it all with them, left on his own at times for quite long periods but never forgotten.

He had been on his own last October when the news broke that the surprise weekend in Paris that Peter had planned to celebrate Susan's 40th birthday had ended in a car accident with both critically injured. Theo had been there waiting for her when she came home weeks later, still in plaster, and alone – more alone than he'd ever known her. For months the piano sat silent, the music collection amassed over the years untouched and Peter's absence was an open wound that nothing could heal. Even he could not find a way to help. But, a year later, she was singing again and chatting to him in the old way, not just existing from day to day.

Now she was leaving the old life behind, moving from the cottage into a tiny flat in the city. Nearer to her new teaching post at the Conservatoire was all she had said, but the move to town seemed to have lifted her spirits amazingly.

Glancing round the room, his eyes fell on the pile of envelopes and a small parcel that she had dropped on the chair.

Back into the room she came, carrying a tray set with mugs, biscuits and a brimming cafetiere. "With all the fuss, I bet you thought I'd forgotten," she said, putting down the tray and lifting the mail. "Three letters for me and a special parcel for you!" As he watched, she tore open the wrapping to reveal a magnificent red silk waistcoat. Holding it up for him to admire, she said, "I had it made for you as I'm not the seamstress gran was. A new beginning for you too. Come, try it on."

Helping him into the waistcoat, she said somewhat shyly, "I've never really told you how special you are to me. You've helped me through so many things – always there when I needed you. I do love you so." As she spoke, the doorbell rang. "Oh, and I've got another surprise for you," she said and skipped out of the room.

He heard her open the front door and soon a good-looking man of about 45 was ushered into the room, self-consciously clutching a large bunch of flowers

"For you," he said, scanning the room. "Hope you haven't already packed all the vases."

"Oh, they're beautiful." She kissed his cheek. Theo saw the glow of happiness in her eyes. So this was why she was singing again; why she was leaving the old sadness behind.

"I'm only taking what I'll really need for the flat, nothing more. But I'm forgetting myself. John, this is Theo, my oldest friend." She smiled, "Theo, John is buying the cottage. He's asked me to share it with him," she blushed, "so I'll be back every weekend to enjoy its tranquillity."

Taking hold of Susan's hand, the man said, "I've heard a lot about you, Theo, and your life here. Chestnut Cottage has always been your home, so how could I expect you to leave after a hundred years?"

Susan glanced lovingly at the man by her side as she cradled the handsome Steiff bear in the brand new silk waistcoat.

Remembrance

by Helena Sheridan

And now, that sacred silence falls,
When blood red poppies rain,
This grieving heart once more recalls,
The anguish and the pain.

But where amid this shower lies,
That solitary bloom,
For which this lonely widow cries,
Beside the martyr's tomb?

Here? In this bright vermilion storm,
This clustered crimson mass,
That renders neither name nor form,
But silently slips past?

And still the gentle petals come,
To mark the bitter cost,
For each a father, daughter, son,
But where the love I've lost?

How in this splendid pageantry,
This regimental plan,
Can I remember, quietly,
My ordinary man?

Shocking!

by Maggie Bolton

The salon doorbell clanged as a customer left. Mavis Astbury rustled her magazine, an indignant look puckering her face.

"Did you see that?" she said, "...her that just went out – did you see the state of her hair? Shocking pink it was. Shocking pink – I ask you!"

Before her friend Betty could answer, Lois, the young hair-stylist came bustling through.

"OK there Betty? Five more minutes and then Jean will rinse you off," she said on her way past, "I'll be with you in a minute Mrs Astbury. I've just got Mrs Flynn's blow-dry and then it's you, OK? Sorry, we're running a bit late this afternoon."

Mavis Astbury's face puckered even more.

"I suppose it will have to be OK, won't it?" she said, adding quite loudly to her friend, "Time was you'd get a nice cup of tea while you were waiting. That seems to have gone by the board. It's all this make-over nonsense now – no time for cups of tea apparently."

"Didn't you see who that was with the pink hair?" Betty said, leaning closer, "It was Josie Cotterell – you know, her that used to be Josephine McGonagall."

"Josephine Mc... It never was. Josephine McGonagall is older than you and me for heaven's sake and that woman looked... No, you're wrong. It couldn't have been her," Mavis said, flicking crossly through her magazine.

"Ah, but it was though," said Betty with a smug look, "I was just speaking to her before you came in. Been through a messy divorce you know – very sad. He went off with some woman half his age."

"Typical," Mavis said, "That's men for you."

"Yes, she was very depressed for a while but, do you know, she said actually it was probably the best thing that's ever happened to her."

"What? She never!" Mavis said, laying the magazine aside.

"Yes, she says now she can be – what was it? Oh yes, she can be true to herself instead of being what someone else wants her to be."

Mavis looked doubtful. "That's her being true to herself then is it – pink hair?" she said, "I don't think so. I always thought she was a dull, dowdy bit of a thing – looked as if she'd dressed out of the rag-bag or borrowed off her granny."

"Well," said Betty, "that would be down to her mother I expect – proper little Hitler she was. Poor Josephine never stood a chance. Anyway, she decided to take control of her life she said, so she had one of them make-overs. There's a girl comes here on Wednesdays and advises you on clothes and make-up and – you know – life-style and that, just like on the telly. Lois does your hair and nails and there you are. Josie says she feels like a new woman – certainly looks like one."

"Good gracious, whatever next?"

"...and being a new woman," Betty continued with a smirk, "She felt like a new man. Ha, ha! So she went out and got one."

"What?" Mavis said, "At her age? Why that's ... that's absolutely..."

"...brilliant! Yes, I thought so. He loves the pink hair apparently, so she just popped in for a booster on the colour. They're off on holiday tomorrow – Monte Carlo."

Their conversation was interrupted as Betty was whisked away for her hair wash. Mavis picked up the magazine again but she turned the pages unseeing, her thoughts elsewhere. Josephine McGonagall of all people: who would have thought it?"

"Right, Mrs Astbury," said Lois at last, "so what can we do for you today? The usual is it – shampoo and set?"

Mavis Astbury frowned, her prim mouth set in a thin, determined line.

"No," she said, "today I think I'll have a pink rinse and I'd like an appointment for Wednesday please."

The Way We Were

by Fiona Atchison

Cover me in swathes of love
Embellish me with gold
Kiss me deeply on the lips
Ignore my getting old

We made a vow upon a day
Now you choose to ignore
Your promise was to honour me
To cherish and adore

My face reflects the type of life
Led through the passing years
Laughter lines, to smile about
Some deeper with the tears

Children born from our young love
Brought joy, from where we'd lain
Come to me with tender eyes
So we can be again

Years hang loose upon my bones
Longing tugs my heart
You are but a beat away
Yet moving more apart

Listen to my sentiments
A yearning for the past
Take the hand I offer you
Our love was meant to last

—

I cover you in swathes of love
Embellish you with gold
I kiss you deeply on the lips
Ignore your getting old

Know I'll care for you my girl
Until I can no more
Till every breath has been and gone
From out my very core

The Boy Next Door

by Janice Johnston

I watched the sun rise over the trees – an autumnal pumpkin sending cinematic happy-ending gold over the town. It was going to be a beautiful day. I was glad. I wanted Adam's day to be beautiful.

The gardens below my bedroom window were still in shadow. Dad and Adam's dad had built a proper fence to separate them now. When we were growing up, the old fence had merely marked the boundary. Adam and I quickly realised we could each double our play area by ignoring it. We climbed over it, crawled under it, kicked footballs through it, and bounced tennis balls against it until the fence gave up any pretence of separating our gardens. It might as well try and separate Adam and me. Eventually our fathers decided to remove the fence.

"But I want to help!" I sulked.

"Off to your room, missy. We'll all get along a lot faster if we don't have to keep an eye on you!" Dad had long since worked out that any mischief Adam and I got up to had usually been devised by me.

The easiest way to take down the fence safely was to remove me from the area. "Adam, you can choose – stay out of the way with Katy, or help your dad – what's it to be?"

It was no choice, really.

"It's not fair!" I stomped off to my bedroom alone to peer out of the window when I thought no one would notice.

47

Every time Adam caught sight of me he jumped up and down waving chunks of wood and laughing. I slid down the wall to sit on the floor. I tasted salty tears mixed with the smell of burning wood and sun-baked roses. I hated Adam.

Then he screamed – a steel blade of sound cutting right to my soul. For a second I couldn't breathe. My lungs were full of wood smoke and perfumed roses and my head full of Adam's pain.

"Kathryn! Breakfast's ready." Mum's voice wavered slightly over the familiar words. I breathed again and pulled myself back to the present. My room felt empty today. Usually Jeff would share it with me, our two boys in the bedroom across the hall. The boys would clatter downstairs, fight over breakfast cereals, and seem so much bigger in my parents' small semi than in our house. This time I'd come alone. I missed them, missed the distraction of their lives, but I knew I needed to be here on my own.

Dad smiled as I sat down at the kitchen table but his eyes scrutinised me carefully, "OK, love?"

"I was just thinking about the day you took down the fence"

This time the smile was genuine. "If there was a hole to fall down, or something to trip over, or a nail to stand on you could be sure Adam'd be there. I've never known such a clumsy boy." He laughed.

"I'd to go with him to Casualty." I rubbed my hand as if I could still feel his fingers digging into my palm as they removed the nail. He wouldn't let me go.

—

"Yes," Dad looked serious again, "You always did look after him."

"Not all the time." I sighed, picking at the food in front of me.

He gripped my hand on our first day at school, too.

"Look after Adam, pet." My mother stroked my hair then pushed the pair of us towards the classroom. Not, "Adam, look after Kathryn." Even then we all knew I was the strong one. I turned to watch Mum and Adam's mum walk out of the school. Adam's mum turned, gave a wobbly smile and waved. Adam clutched my hand even tighter.

As I dressed and applied mascara with an almost steady hand, I thought about Adam's schooldays.

"No, look." Adam prised the pencil from my hand and began to scribble on the notepad. "You have to do this bit first, then the rest is easy." His fingers flew over the paper and a beautifully neat explanation of the maths problem appeared on the page.

"Easy for you, maybe." I rubbed my forehead and tried to follow his reasoning. Numbers had always been easy for Adam.

His eyes lit up when we learned our times tables. "Four times four is sixteen, four times five is twenty" the class would chant, almost in unison. I was always that beat behind.

He counted all the time; railings round the school, bricks in a wall, steps between our homes and the swings. He loved working things out with the numbers he collected. "Did you know that it's the same number of steps from here to the station as it is from here to the church?" He looked up, expecting me to be as fascinated as he was. When he wasn't working out sums and angles for fun, he'd take apart pieces of machinery then put them back together again.

Sometimes they worked, sometimes they didn't. His dad was furious when he took apart the lawnmower. Adam had to borrow ours for the rest of the summer to cut both lawns. But by the next spring he had his dad's lawnmower working again, better than before.

I stood in the hall and brushed some fluff from my shoulder. It was my favourite suit but the soft wool showed the least little thing.

Mum bustled through. "It's not time to set off already, is it?" She looked back into the kitchen as if mentally listing everything she had to do before leaving.

"It's OK." I smiled. "It's such a nice day I thought I'd walk. You and dad follow on later in the car."

I walked to the school. It took fewer steps than it had when we were younger. I still counted them, for Adam. At the gates I looked across to the meadow, a wilderness beyond the school. We'd spent hours playing on the rough ground, carrying planks of wood to build a den, and bread and jam for a picnic.

Of course, it wasn't a meadow now. Meadowside Crescent and Oak Park and Holly Way sprouted up after we left primary school. I still saw the tussocks of grass and patchy hedges that had made up our very own adventure playground.

"I'm going to be an engineer when I grow up." He told me as we ate blackberries pulled from the hedgerow. We must have been six, maybe seven, at the time. I hadn't thought of growing up. I thought we'd stay aged six, maybe seven, be in Mrs Jenkins's class, and eat blackberries forever.

"What's an engineer?" I asked suspiciously.

"Someone who takes things apart, fixes them, then puts them back together again so they work better than before." He smiled.

"What sort of things?"

"Cars, maybe aeroplanes, maybe huge ginormous tanks. Anything." He sighed expectantly at the thought of all that taking apart and putting back together again.

I walked on up the hill and thought about Jeff and Adam, how different they were. I'd tried to explain to him about my relationship with Adam.

"He was my first love, you see. You never forget your first love no matter how badly it ends." I nursed the glass of red wine Jeff had poured. "We fitted together perfectly. We grew up together, helped ourselves to biscuits from each other's kitchen. We laughed at the same things. Even across the classroom, he could glance at me and know what I was thinking." I stared into the distance, remembering. "It was only when we took things further that it didn't work.

—

"I think everyone expected us to become boyfriend and girlfriend so we went along with it. I wish we hadn't." I closed my eyes and sighed. "In trying to change our relationship we lost a big chunk of our friendship."

"Like one of those jigsaws." Jeff sipped his wine.

"What do you mean?"

"You know those jigsaws that have totally different pictures on each side?"

"That's it." I sat up, almost knocking over the bottle on the table. "The friendship picture was perfect. The pieces had been beside each other so long they'd almost knitted together. Then we flipped it over, tried to make up the new picture. It had to be put together piece by piece. We expected it to be easy – after all, we had all the bits – but somehow they didn't fit together the same way. Then, when we tried to go back to being just friends, we found there were pieces missing, the fit wasn't as tight, it wasn't the same." I took a gulp of wine and sank back down into the cushions. "By that time we were glad to be heading off to universities at different ends of the country."

At the top of the hill I stopped to catch my breath and look over the town. I seemed to remember it being bigger when we were young.

He would send me e-mails.

"We studied sprockets today." He'd write, or some other equally boring engineering term. You could tell he loved the course work. When I wrote back about wild parties, sleeping on floors, missing lectures, he would be almost bewildered. It was a bit like maths and me all those years ago. Adam had helped me then.

I wasn't there to hold his hand this time, to help him become part of the crowd, the sort of person who would think of going to wild parties and missing lectures. Adam could only stand on the outside.

Then he found some new friends. They helped him stay up all night to study. They helped him relax after exams. Then he stopped e-mailing me.

We lost touch after that. I guess I was too involved with Jeff to worry about Adam. I knew he'd had problems finding work after graduating and eventually had come back home to stay with his parents.

I could picture so clearly the last time I spoke to him.

Mum met us at the station.

"Oh, pet, it's so good to see you." Mum's embrace gathered up the two boys and me in one great hug. "Such a shame Jeff couldn't come, too." She released us all, then studied the boys carefully. "I think you've both grown at least six inches since you were last here."

"It's not that long, Mum." I hauled out our bags.

"Oh, I didn't mean to nag you. It's just they seem to grow so fast." She grabbed a bag. "Let's get you home. Now, who likes chocolate cake?"

"Me, me!" Clamoured the boys.

"And me!" I laughed.

—

We walked home, the boys running ahead, me watching for hazards, but it was a quiet street with a wide pavement. Then, up ahead, I saw a drunk staggering out of the corner shop.

"Back here, boys." I made to shepherd them across the road.

Mum stopped chattering. "You go on." She shoved my bag into my hands. "I'll see you later." She marched determinedly up the road.

"Mum, wait." I caught up with her. "You can't go near that drunk, you don't know what he might do."

Mum bit her lip. I could see her eyes filling with tears. She took a deep breath. "Kathryn, it's Adam."

"Adam? It can't be." I forgot about my children, about my mother and remembered my best friend.

As I approached, I recognised his stance, his thick hair that would never lie flat, but I didn't recognise my Adam.

"Adam?"

At the sound of my voice, he half sobered up immediately. By the look on his face, he didn't want me to see him like this. I wished I didn't have to see him like this, either.

"Katy?" He tried so hard not to slur. "Just having a little celebration."

From the state of him it was obvious this celebration had been going on for a long time. His body was bloated, his clothes grubby, he looked at least 15 years older than me.

"Can I walk you home?" I made to take his arm. I wanted to get him away from any more alcohol.

"No, no." He turned away, waving his hand in my direction. "I have to meet some friends." He made a great show of studying his watch. "Good to see you again." And he walked off down the lane, carefully placing one foot in front of the other.

"Adam, wait!"

He didn't turn, but one arm came up in a final gesture of farewell.

And that was the last time I spoke to him. Oh, I tried but he wouldn't see me again.

"He's too embarrassed." Adam's mum poured me a coffee in her kitchen next morning. "He didn't want you to know how low he's sunk."

"But can't we do something? A clinic, different doctors, anything?"

Adam's mum shook her head. "We've tried. We've been trying for years. He's got to want to stop or it's no use."

"But surely he doesn't want to be like this." I automatically helped myself to a biscuit from the tin.

"He doesn't, and he has stopped. Three times he's managed to give up the drink and drugs. He's started new jobs, too, but they're usually far away from here. He's stuck in a bedsit on his own, can't make new friends so he turns to his old ones again." She closed her eyes and a tear slid slowly down her cheek. "I dread going into his bedroom, now, in case I find him dead." She sighed," Then, sometimes, I wish he was dead, at least he'd be at peace."

I was on the final stretch now, top of the hill then down to the church. Adam would remember exactly how many steps but he wouldn't be walking it today.

—

55

I waited till most people had left the graveyard before hugging Adam's mum and dad.

"I can't believe he's not here anymore."

"He's been gone for a long time now, Katy." Adam's dad squeezed my shoulders. "We all tried to help him back. Oh, he would make an effort for a while, fight the weight, plan to have a future, then something would set him back, he'd lose track. He trusted the drugs and alcohol more than he trusted himself. He wasn't strong enough to fight them forever."

I walked back through the graveyard. The gardener was raking up leaves and burning fallen branches. For a second I couldn't breathe. My lungs were full of wood smoke and perfumed roses and my head full of Adam's pain, just like in our back gardens a long, long time ago.

But Adam's pain was over now. He'd never need me to hold his hand again. "Be at peace," I whispered, watching the wisps of wood smoke drift skywards. Closing my eyes, I said goodbye to the boy next door.

The Professional

by Greta Yorke

She's a siren, a beauty who prostitutes for self-gratification. With scarlet hour-glass figure and shapely slender legs she plies her patch with regularity. Scantily clad she waits for action; new tricks fall for her allure each time, such is the power of her attraction.

Although they know her form, she charms and they submit to this dominatrix. They can't see beyond her shiny veneer. Innate instinct draws them to her, what male's going to resist? When she's satisfied they're expendable. She eats them up and spits them out, treacherous black widow.

Connect Two

by Lesley Deschner

Sunlight bathed our bodies
- no other warmth required:
and through the open window,
we ignored the sounds outside.
I smiled, caressed your skin and traced a downward
path with my fingers.
You smiled and reached for me.

Passion fuelled our movements
- no other thought in mind:
and through our wanton pleasure,
we indulged our fantasy.
I sighed, and held you closer, and pushed the outside
world away from me.
You sighed and kissed my mouth.

Friendship masked our goodbyes
- no more a loving touch:
and through our daily living,
returns our reality.
I smiled and let you go, and assured myself it would
be enough.
You smiled, and walked away.

Laughter hides my sorrow
- no, there are no regrets:
and though my heart stays with you,
I know it can never be.
I weep, and think of you,
and close my eyes to remember your touch.
I weep and think of you.

—

Yellow Stars

by Fiona Atchison

It was a dying buzzard that drew us to the rubble. Trapped against an iron grille, its legs were shattered. When we approached, one dark wing hovered slightly. It will die soon, I remember my mother saying. Even if it broke free it could never hunt again. So it was not only our desperate need but a kindness that compelled her to take the delicate neck and firmly squeeze. I whispered a blessing under my breath as she instructed, my eyes closed. But I peeked as did Rena, though we never spoke of it again. We had to eat, mother said, the three of us had to survive, for father's sake.

When the bird no longer obscured the grille, mother peered through the narrow bars. She turned, excitement evident in her expression and beckoned us forward. As my eyes adjusted to the murky depths, I began to make out shapes and understood mother's unusual animation. The main house must have imploded upon bomb impact, yet down below was a cellar, seemingly intact apart from a dense layer of debris.

Satisfied there were no other access points in the remains, mother said, "Samuel, if we can prise this grille off then I'll lower you down to see what can be salvaged."

So Rena and mother set about working at the edges with rusted tools stolen from a farm, whilst I prodded ineffectively with father's old penknife, my prized possession. She would halt us from time to time, listening, intensely alert. The Polish

---

59

countryside, dense with forest, provided good cover but at the bomb site we were more visible. We hadn't spoken to anyone in many weeks by that time. Mother indoctrinated us with her daily mantra, 'only trust one another, and always keep hidden'. Up until that point, we had.

The grille began to loosen, taking all three of us finally to force it free. Mother lay flat and poked her head through the opening, her shoulders wedged at an angle. We waited impatiently before she withdrew. We were still children, we were excited and so without thinking, raised our voices, "What can you see, Mama?"

Immediately, she motioned us to quieten. We held our breath. There was a distant crunch of something heavy stirring the air until it became more steadfast, treading our way. Without warning, mother's violent grip forced me head first through the hole. Many feet from the ground I dropped, landing roughly, arms pulled instinctively over my skull. From this foetal position, urgent whispers between my mother and sister penetrated down. Then Rena's feet and legs appeared until, with a soft slither, she fell beside me. We knew better than to utter another sound. Rena gazed up at the square of daylight frantic with worry. We stared in growing alarm as the grille was lodged back in place. Then the gasping of our mother hauling stones until all light vanished and we were confined and alone in a black hole. For long minutes we waited. All silent but for the liquid dark of our own breathing.

"The hole is too small for mother but she'll be back when it's safe." Rena tried to reassure me but I heard tears in her whisper. Her hand sought mine.

Gradually the blackness subsided as our eyes adjusted. Tiny chinks of light pierced through the gloom, revealing bulky shadows. It was a damp place, much colder than the June evening above. No matter, we were hidden and hopefully safe.

My thoughts, as they often did when I felt frightened, strayed back to my father and his disappearance. A freezing night in January 1942 and father was very late returning home to our lodgings in the Lodz Ghetto. As a postman he had many privileges. In his uniform he could ride a bike outside the ghetto to the main city streets. He brought home extra rations and was in good standing within our own Jewish community. Sometimes he brought back bad news, but at least it was news of outside. That particular evening, as he was cycling in a poor area of the city, he was suddenly stopped and taken by a German patrol along with some other men. The party was marched to a wooded area and ordered to dig a pit many feet wide and deep. They were to dig their own graves before a firing squad.

From then our conditions worsened and we depended on the charity of relations and our meagre bread ration to survive. We were forced to make many hiding places during our last few months in the ghetto as the German SS kept arriving in cattle trucks during the night. They rounded up children, the old, the ill and weak. Mother always insisted we wear our best clothes concealed by our old ones on top. As was inevitable, we amongst many others were finally discovered and hounded into these open trucks, clutching our precious belongings.

Now, trapped in the dark, I feared for my mother. What if she had been caught, perhaps taken back to the railway? I still had nightmares from that train journey. At first the wagon we'd been squashed into smelled merely of strong disinfectant and wasting bodies. But as the stifling journey progressed, the stench and conditions became more and more unbearable. I witnessed many old people unable to use the buckets provided as makeshift toilets. Later, it hadn't mattered as they soon overflowed. Some of the adults stood silent, some prayed; others wailed at the rumours of our destination. But as the train slowed, a deathly silence descended.

It halted at Treblinka Station. A few minutes of absolute hush, then came the crashing of truck doors sliding open one by one. Like a horde of mute quivering animals, we were pressed onto the platform to a confusion of glaring lights, barking dogs and soldiers shouting orders. In this mayhem, I witnessed my mother manage to retain an amazing self-control. Ducking to her knees she pulled our old and dirty clothing off, crawled through the jumble of legs, slid down onto the track pulling us after her. We continued to crawl desperately under the train, the screaming and begging voices of our countrymen coming from above. We kept going until mother whispered us to stop. She got us to crouch, then she brushed herself down and pinned her hat back on. She took a chance and peeked over the platform.

Almost immediately a deep voice cried, "Hey! what are you doing there? You – go back!" A figure was tramping briskly in our direction.

Mother with her Aryan features and fine tailored clothing, turned sharply. Now we no longer had a yellow star on our jackets to pinpoint us as Jews, she spoke as if she belonged there.

"Is it any of your business that my children needed some air? We were waiting in the car for my husband, Herr Schultz." She indicated with her head to where a black Daimler sat at the railway entrance. The porter wavered for many seconds, then thought better of it.

He tipped his cap. "Apologies" and offered his hand to assist her onto the platform.

We had then walked hand in hand with as much dignity as our shaking legs would lend towards the looming Daimler. Aware of the porter's eyes stalking us, our luck held. The car was empty and the rear door clicked open. Enclosed in the leather interior we soon became overwhelmingly conscious of the smell of human waste clinging to our shoes. It was then mother realised as she stared at the porter's stalwart back, that he had not been fooled for one second. In silence, we ran from the car towards a darkly forested hill, my mother whispering a prayer for the man who had just saved us.

The cellar was crammed with disused furniture. It was hard to negotiate without banging knees or dislodging mounds of dirt. Rena eventually jarred open a dresser drawer and carefully dipped her hand inside. A sweet smell rose, making my stomach contract with hunger. Rena sniffed at the oval object she had removed.

"It's *kolacz* I think", she whispered to me, and cautiously nibbled. "The bread's stale but still sweet. Samuel, eat some and put the rest in your pocket."

We fell asleep on a table, shivering and huddled together. I awoke thirsty, longing for a drink from the stream above. My eyes fell upon rows of muck filled bottle racks. I may have been only seven years old, but I recognised wine when I saw it, so nudged Rena awake. As thirsty as we were, the bitter red liquid caused our faces to contort. We sniggered until our bony frames convulsed with soundless laughter. A new bravado entered our veins. We heaved the table round until positioned under the grille. Levering herself onto the table top Rena then bent down and I clambered onto her shoulders. The seriousness of our situation settled on us once more. With spindly arms I leaned hard in to the grille, my fingers gripping the bars. Nothing budged. I could smell the scented breeze from outside drift through cracks in the rocks. It made me desperate for freedom.

"It won't move Rena, we're trapped," my voice rose.

We exchanged places. I leaned my back against the wall, Rena stood on my shoulders. She was eleven and light as a leaf, her legs so thin they could snap. Even so I began to buckle and she wavered precariously before jumping down. Looking frantically around, Rena stopped and banged her forehead with the heel of her palm.

"Are we stupid? Help me lift up this chair, Samuel."

I held the chair firm as Rena began straining against the grille. After a series of loud gasps I realised she was using her broken screwdriver to hack at the blockage. What felt like hours later, the chair slid with a simultaneous muffled clatter of dislodging stones. Miraculously the cellar was infused with daylight. Like a circus act I balanced on the chair and scrabbled my way out. Rena passed up some wine bottles and a few useful looking implements, then hauled herself though the gap. We lay down catching our breath in relief, squinting at the sun. But as our eyes adjusted and fear replaced our brief sense of release, we noticed with a start – we had company.

Drawn by our noise, a band of runaways, all children much like ourselves hovered over us. They were ragged and thin but each armed with a weapon.

"What were you doing down there?" demanded the eldest looking boy. He held a hand pistol pointed directly at Rena's head. His eyes were calculating as he stowed our wine in a sack. Rena hauled me to my feet, her face white.

"Hiding from the Germans. What are you doing here?"

Yet instead of waiting for the boy's answer, to my horror Rena lunged at the head of a small blond girl. No longer afraid now, she was screeching.

"This is my mother's hat, how did she get it?"

Rena then ran at the boy, punching him hard in the stomach. Two younger children grabbed her arms, whilst another came for me. The winded boy slumped on the grass.

"Listen, I can tell you," he gasped, "just let me get my breath and promise not to do that again."

Rena nodded and he indicated the others to let us be.

I sat close to my sister as he told us, "My name is Peter. We've been travelling and trying to survive in these forests for many weeks now. We've learned to avoid the peasants living around here because they can't be trusted. Some are making money by handing us over to the German patrols..."

I felt alarmed by his words and their implications and shouted, "Have you seen our mother?"

Peter did not reply but motioned Rena to sit beside him. He whispered in her ear and when he was done, Rena held herself and cried. Without our mother to guide and protect us, we joined with the other children.

Those memories are now a lifetime away. I sit with my grandson in my daughter Anya's house in England. Sunshine spills through the conservatory windows. There is much more for me to tell him but that is enough for today. Eventually he will learn about his Aunt Rena whom he's never met who, alongside a brave boy called Peter, saved many of those children yet were unable to save themselves.

I turn at the sound of Anya approaching with a large tray of tea and biscuits. She looks questioningly at me and I nod. Young Peter's face is grave and unusually for him he does not jump to grab something from the plate. Instead he is staring at an old penknife handed down from my father to me. He is just seven years old.

"Papa, the story, is it ... did it really happen?"

Anya, pouring tea, answers for me, "All that Papa told you is true, and so we must always remember that very bad time and the family we lost. Do you understand what I mean Peter?"

—

He nods his head and slowly hands me back the penknife, "You said you'll look after it for me until I'm older. You won't forget – will you Papa?"

"No," I reply, "I will never forget."

Family Ties

by Catherine Lang

"Have we met?"
A whisper, paper thin.
A weak, uncertain smile
touches pursed lips, no further,
as empty eyes rake features mirrored in her own.

Thin light through grimy panes reveals
a shabby, flat pack room.
The curled up edges of a long forgotten life
litter each surface.
Lost in dust.

The ebon sun-cracked desk alone stands proud,
a silent echo of a bustling life.
Around, the stifling scent of unkempt age,
while faded roses droop
with mildewed blooms, untouched.

She hums in tuneless discord,
unheeding of her guest.
A raw-boned cat demands the vacant lap,
as work-worn fingers
pluck lint from shapeless cotton.

A family smiles, lopsided
behind cracked glass.
A soldier, housewife, child.
A final cherished summer, unremembered,
time ticking blankly by.

—

The soldier's grandchild stands.
Fresh lips brush parchment skin.
The sitter raises, tilts her grizzled head.
Eyes brighten, almost shine.
"I should know you."

Lost & Found

by Greta Yorke

The holiday was over and it was with real regret that Sharon piled the cases and bags onto the trolley with a mind of its own and headed as best she could towards the terminal building. Ryan and Katie followed their mother closely while Harry was tethered to the trolley with a wrist strap. As they reached the terminal entrance a bus decanted passengers and luggage into a chaotic maelstrom, which gathered Sharon and her brood and spewed them through the doors and into the heaving reception area. Glad to have survived the crush, Sharon's ears were pierced by wails from Harry.

"Where's my bunny?" he cried.

This rabbit had been a birthday present from his dad, who had left the family six months earlier having found his 'soul mate' in the form of 24-year-old PA, Zoe. Jack's Eureka moment apparently happened somewhere between Sharon's morning sickness and stretch marks attributed to the now three-year-old Harry.

Sharon hadn't realised it would be quite so difficult organising three children for their first trip without their father. By the time she had washed, ironed and packed their clothes she was more ready for a spa break than two weeks in a villa with 'the gang'.

The taxi had arrived and Ryan 11, Katie 9 and Harry tumbled in, leaving Sharon to struggle with

---

cases and bags. The dreaded two hour wait for departure was less stressful than anticipated with the older two occupied with electronic games and Harry busy colouring and playing dominoes with mum.

The flight was uneventful, apart from Harry losing his rabbit. Thankfully a couple sitting across the aisle spotted it further down the plane. They chatted to the older children, letting them play games on their electronic pad, which were apparently much better than the ones they had.

Palma was buzzing as Sharon organised the cases and Harry on a trolley. With Ryan and Katie helping, she pushed her way to car rentals and was soon heading north to peace and tranquillity. Off the main road and down a potholed track Sharon manoeuvred the car through the gates of their villa. The air conditioning in the car didn't prepare them for the breath-taking air outside and Sharon struggled once more with the luggage. Thankfully thick stone walls and air conditioning guaranteed coolness indoors.

The children were desperate to test the pool, so priority was given to finding swimwear. Ryan and Katie were able swimmers and thrashed about like fish while Harry was quite happy to bob about in his swim jacket as Sharon pushed and pulled him through the water. The children's shrieks were joyous; this was summer heaven. Hunger eventually brought them inside to raid the fridge of its cold meats, yoghurts and fruit, eaten with chunks of crusty bread. When they finished, Sharon unpacked while the children complained about not being allowed in the pool unsupervised. This was another time Jack would have been handy.

After she had emptied the cases Sharon settled the children in the car and off they went to explore the town and do some food shopping.

They walked through cobbled streets bustling with a night market. There were colourful stalls selling all imaginable things, bags, jewellery, shoes, clothes. Noses indulged on paella, sugared nuts, olives and spit roasted chickens. The children gawped at stilt walkers and fire eaters and were most reluctant to leave for the supermarket. Thankfully it was well stocked with reliable favourites and the trolley soon strained with sugary cereals, burgers, pizza, chips and baked beans.

In darkness they returned to the villa where the children resumed their games as Sharon dealt with the shopping then moved beds around so that they could all sleep in one room. One by one the children climbed into bed and Sharon settled in the easy chair with her book and a glass of Shiraz. Bliss.

The first week passed quickly with only a trip to the market interrupting the pleasures of the villa and pool. There were orange and lemon trees in the garden and the children helped Sharon to make lemonade and orange juice. Then the weather changed and black clouds crept towards the villa. The rain which followed was torrential and lasted all day restricting play to indoor. That evening the wind picked up bringing thunder and all kinds of lightning. Branches battered against their window and Harry and Katie cuddled closer into Sharon with each crack and bang. Ryan refused to concede and turned up the volume on his MP3 player. Then there was one almighty crack and the electricity went off.

Thankfully it was near bedtime so Sharon lit a candle and shepherded them upstairs.

Next day the storm continued with rivers cascading down the hillside behind the villa. That's when the moaning started. All entertainment required charging, the children were 'bored'.

Sharon gathered paper and coloured pens and pencils from the dresser drawer and introduced them to Hangman, joining dots and a drawing game on folded paper which created weird and hilarious results, they played Charades. Harry watched with his rabbit and colouring book to occupy him. The bookcase was well stocked and had a selection of board games. Sharon set out 'Frustration' which Harry could play, developing his counting skills without realising.

Luckily there was plenty of tinned food, fruit and vegetables. With bread from the freezer, crisps and nuts they had plenty to eat. The children discovered they quite liked this new healthy diet which delighted Sharon.

They had three days of this before the electricity was restored. During that time a closeness developed which probably wouldn't have had the power cut not occurred. There was much laughter and giggling.

The pool resembled a great citrus cocktail, oranges and lemons bobbed among the floating leaves. Ryan helped Sharon to fish the debris out using nets and thankfully the sun returned for the rest of their holiday. They bought gifts at the market, swam in the sea and each night they played 'Frustration' before bed. There were tears when it was time to leave the villa but everyone helped as Sharon squeezed the cases into the hire car.

Now the family looked frantically around the airport foyer but the rabbit was gone. Harry wailed his way towards the check-in and security. As they approached the snaking cordoned area the man from their outward flight pushed up beside them.

"I think this might be yours," he said holding out the familiar rabbit. Harry grabbed it and buried his face in its fur, still sobbing.

"Thank you so much," sighed Sharon, "I really thought he'd gone for good this time!"

"I heard the crying at the entrance then recognised the rabbit under a seat. I'm glad I spotted it," he continued joining them in the queue.

Sharon had to prise the rabbit from Harry when they reached the scanner. He watched through flowing tears as his rabbit disappeared into the machine.

"It's alright," Sharon reassured, "watch and you'll see him come out the other end."

And he did. And the man turned out to be Ben who'd accompanied his sister to her new teaching post in Palma. As they waited for the flight to be called Ben stayed with them, chatting to Sharon and helping the children play the games.

Back home Sharon declared a new rule, no television or electronic games between dinner and bedtime, everyone would help to wash and tidy up after the meal, that way they would spend more time together.

That was over a month ago. Today after Jack called for the children Sharon ignored housework. Instead she busied herself getting ready for a lunch date, with Ben.

—

Visiting Time

A narrative poem by Fiona McFadzean

He visits on Sundays. A big hard man,
no space on arms or body for another tattoo.
To her he is just Daddy. She runs towards him
to be swung high in the air, hugs him tight,
kisses his cheek, mindful of the piercings.

"The school trip was awesome, Daddy.
We went in a bus to a Centre away up the Clyde."
He grunts, settles at the table, her class project
laid out for him to see. "We learned loads an' loads
about badgers an' otters, an' birds an' insects
and loads else." He grunts again

"We had to choose just one to write about, Daddy,
so I picked the badger." She lifts the postcard, lays it
gently against her face before putting it in his hand.
"See, Daddy, it's got a black face with a white stripe
an' a grey body with a wee tail.
An' its front paws are strong 'cause it's got to dig up
plants an' worms an' things for eating.
Isn't it just cute, Daddy?"

He grins, points to its face before answering
"Looks like it follows Ayr United."
"Oh, Daddy," she giggles and punches his arm.
"You are so funny and I love you. Cuddle, please."
"Love you, too, Princess." His voice is husky
as he clasps her firmly to his chest. "But I wish we
could be like the badgers," she whispers.

"Do you know loads of families live together? They
burrow under the ground, make houses called setts,
keep their babies safe, don't need to foster them."

He sighs. "That would be great, Princess. I truly wish
we were Badgers." "No you don't." She giggles
and punches again.
"You'd lose your street cred with all your gangs
if you looked like you followed Ayr United. You're a
Glasgow man."
He ruffles her riot of blond curls. "Sure am
Princess."

The doorbell rings. She squeals with joy.
"It's the pizza man, Daddy. We're having our
favourite, Mrs Jo ordered it special."
"I'll have mine without worms," he manages to say
over the lump in his throat, "seeing I'm not a
badger."
"Yuk, Daddy. Me, too." Her voice wobbles. "Though
I still wish we could be badgers." He doesn't answer,
just takes the box from Mrs Jo, nods his thanks,
before she returns to the kitchen, leaving the door
open as usual.

They eat, take small bites, trying to make time pass
as slowly as the seven sleeps between visits.
Although it hurts when he goes there will be
no tears. In the two years since her fifth birthday
she has learned not to cry.
He will head for the pub, a good excuse for a drink.

—
76

Party Girl

A pantoum by Maggie Bolton

She's getting old you know. It's such a shame.
She used to be so vibrant and alive.
Late night parties? She was always game!
But now she's nodding off by half past five.
She used to be so vibrant and alive,
Brim full of new ideas and clever schemes,
But now she's nodding off by half past five.
Perhaps instead she has exciting dreams
Brim full of new ideas and clever schemes.
While living now at this pedestrian pace
Perhaps instead she has exciting dreams.
Smiles of remembered mischief on her face,
While living now at this pedestrian pace.
The weathered skin, well wrinkled, cannot hide
Smiles of remembered mischief on her face;
At ninety, still a teenager inside.
The weathered skin, well wrinkled, cannot hide
Her bright intelligence, her sense of fun;
At ninety, still a teenager inside,
As if upon life's journey just begun.
Her bright intelligence, her sense of fun
Is glowing radiantly within,
As if upon life's journey just begun.
Beauty still trapped beneath the waxen skin,
Is glowing radiantly within.
She waltzes grandly in her dressing-gown;
Beauty still trapped beneath the waxen skin.
Alas, the body clock is winding down.
She waltzes grandly in her dressing-gown.
Late night parties? She was always game!
She's getting old you know. It's such a shame.

—

Moving On

by Janice Johnston

Rob groaned, stretched, and checked the time. Best get up. He'd plenty to do this morning. As he padded through to the kitchen, he was surprised to hear Jen's light footsteps follow him.

"Plenty for me to do this morning, too." She smiled, reaching over to switch on the kettle. They stood silently, backs against the old Aga as they waited for the water to boil.

As Rob sipped his tea he thought about his mother. She'd risen along with his father every morning. The Aga had burned coal then, and there weren't such luxuries as electric kettles.

Mother shivered as she rattled through the ashes and relit the Aga. As soon as the kettle boiled, she infused a pot of tea and took a mug out to father in the byre.

"Thanks, lass," he said, every morning for forty-three years.

"Thanks, lass," said Rob, echoing his father, as he handed his empty mug to Jen. "I'd better get a move on."

"Me, too." Jen gulped down the last of her tea. "I'm hoping to have a pot of soup made and the fire lit before the kids get up."

"Are you keeping them off school?"

"I spoke to the head teacher. She said it was OK, under the circumstances."

Rob pulled on his boiler-suit before trudging out to the milking parlour. He looked round at the stainless steel tubing, computer-operated feeding and milking machine removal systems. His grandfather wouldn't recognise anything – except the cows themselves. How had young Robbie's friend described it? Like the inside of a space ship, that was it.

Well, he knew how to run this space ship. As the cows filtered in, he punched their number into the computer. Their carefully calculated feed rattled down a tube to the bowl in front of each cow. While the cows ate, Rob washed their udders and attached milking machines.

Rob had thought he'd never give up his herd of Ayrshire cattle. They held such strong memories of his father and grandfather.

The door rattled as Jen came in.

"Don't usually see you out here." Rob said.

"You don't mind, do you?" She paused, "I thought I'd keep you company."

Rob scratched the nearest animal's rough flank. "I was just thinking, Faither probably milked this cow's great, great grandmother."

"Add on a few more 'greats' and your grandfather would have milked it." Jen smiled. "Remember the wooden pail and three legged stool we found up in the loft?"

Rob hesitated, the silence stretching and jangling. "We won't have a history in Canada, Jen. Are we doing the right thing?"

"Our history will always be here, we're just moving our base. Us Scots have been emigrating for years," Jen reached out to touch his arm. "We might not have a history in Canada but we'll all have a future, especially the kids."

"A future, aye," Rob shook his head, "I hope to God it's better than the one we'd have here. Faither – and his dad – thought there would always be a future in agriculture. They'll always need food and milk, lad, he'd say. But there are so many rules and regulations now, faither would never be able to follow them."

"They had their own problems when they were running the farm. Your grandfather couldn't have coped with milking all this lot," Jen waved an arm to encompass the hundred cows standing in the collecting area, "not by hand."

She held a hand against the glass jar filling with milk. The warmth spread through her fingers. "And think how much work the women did each day. They'd not swan off to the office for nine o'clock, leaving a pot of soup and a plate of sandwiches for lunch."

Rob waited till the next lot of feed had rattled into the bowls before he spoke. "Don't forget, you come home and sort out all the paperwork. We couldn't have lasted this long without you keeping us right."

"Argh, paperwork. Remember all those forms we'd to fill in to even start the process of emigrating." Jen shook her head. "And speaking of paperwork, I'd better make sure all the animal passports are in order." She moved to the door, "Will you be OK on your own?"

"I'll manage." He kept his face turned away.

Rob waited till another batch of cows had been fed and attached to the milking machines before stepping outside. The sun was just beginning to rise

—

over the hill, giving everything a cinematic, happy-ever-after glow.

The rows of recently steam-cleaned machinery laid out in the top field looked like part of a modern sculpture. He had a strange urge to rearrange them to spell out words – like 'HELP' written in the sand, or 'The End' before the credits of a film – but he couldn't decide exactly what he wanted to say. He sighed, and returned to the parlour.

The milking seemed to speed by; no cows had mastitis, no cows kicked off the milking units, nothing went wrong. Rob was scraping out and washing down the parlour when Jen next looked in.

"Someone to see you," she called.

Rob came to the door and watched as a young man scrambled out of a car and loped over.

"Robert Jackson? I'm Mike Black, your auctioneer for today."

"What's happened to David?" Rob froze. "He was supposed to be here."

"Broken leg, I'm afraid. He tripped over his grandson's toy tractor." The young auctioneer grinned and bounced on his heels, eager to get started. His grin faded slightly as he looked into the parlour. "You haven't milked this morning, have you? Usually..."

"I know." Rob wiped his hands on some paper towels. "Usually, cows aren't milked before a sale. That's why I wanted David. He understood."

"Tell me. Maybe I'll understand, too." Mike tipped his head to one side, waiting.

"Come on, it's breakfast time."

Mike clasped a mug of tea as Rob sat down with toast and honey.

"Tell me," he said again.

Rob took a long drink of orange juice and stared across the table at the young auctioneer. Maybe he would understand.

"I've done my best for those animals all their lives," he began. "I've taught them to drink from a pail. I've watched them skipping out into a field for the first time. I've helped them give birth. I've milked them twice a day since they were about three years old. I don't want their final memories – or my final memories – of their life on this farm to be stressful." He stood up and lifted the teapot from the Aga.

Mike held up his mug and Rob refilled it.

"I've explained all this to David." Rob went on, "I know the cows would look better if their udders were full but it would be very uncomfortable for them. And then to be herded into a pen on their own in front of all those buyers, they'd be stressed. It's bad enough for me, and I know what's happening."

"So, how do you want to do this?" Mike sat forward.

"You announce at the start of the sale that they've been milked. I'll bring the cows forward two or three together and we just take it slowly."

"I can do that," Mike nodded. He pulled out the catalogue of goods for sale. "I thought we'd start in the barn with the small stuff, if that's OK with you."

Rob nodded, not trusting himself to speak. 'The small stuff' probably held the most memories. He'd found a croquet set crammed into a corner of the barn loft. He'd no idea which ancestor had first bought it but he could still hear his grandmother's laughter and feel the sunshine of a long ago day as he and his sister tried to hit the balls with the huge mallets.

The tatty wooden sawdust barrow he used every day had been made by his grandfather and repaired by his father. No one would buy that, unless for firewood.

Jen placed a hand on his shoulder. "There's still time to call it all off. We don't have to go through with it."

Rob could sense Mike holding his breath. Yes, he could stop it. He could cancel the sale, cancel the flight tickets, carry on the way they'd done before. But it wouldn't be the same. Since his mother died last year, only six months after his father, there was nothing to keep him here.

Jen was right. Their future, the kids' future, was in Canada. He felt the weight of indecision slip from his shoulders.

He stood up and hugged Jen, wiping away a tear slipping down her cheek. "Aren't the Canadians keen on Ayrshire cattle, too? We can start again. We'll build up a new herd, make new friends." He walked to the door and held it open. "Come on, let's get started."

Famine

by Helena Sheridan

A brittle tree for sanctuary
The withered woman moans,
Her body writhes uncomfortably
To skirt the scorching stones.
Lean fingers frisk the empty sand
And pluck the dust in vain,
With only tears to quench the land
She sobs for blessed rain.
As beauty fades, without a trace,
And laughter leaves her eyes,
Who stops to stroke that hollow face?
Except the thirsty flies.
With barely breath enough to weep,
She watches victims piled,
Then struggles from that endless sleep
To rock her shrivelled child.
Instinctively she tries to cope,
To ease the gnawing pain,
And searches for the slightest hope
For one forgotten grain.

Just a Little Break

(Translated from Dog-speak by Maggie Bolton)

I should have guessed something was up. They've been putting stuff into squashy boxes and making excited noises for days. Then this morning they put everything into the car. My bed, my ball-on-a-string, my fluffy parrot and my food bowls all went in too. Great, we must be going somewhere exciting, I thought. WRONG! They're going somewhere exciting. Apparently, I'm not invited.

Now they've left me in a house that doesn't smell right with some two-leggers that I don't know. I call out in a panic when they drive away. I stand up on my hind legs at the window so they can see that they've forgotten to take me with them, but they don't look back. I call as loudly as I can and jump up and down. Some things fall off the window ledge and smash as they hit the floor. The stranger two-leggers make soothing noises, but I can tell they're not too pleased about the broken things. Now they've put me in my bed in a place where I can't see out of the window and I'm firmly told to STAY.

So here I am. I'm depressed. I've been lying here for ages and I'm bored, bored, bored. Wait a minute, someone's coming. It's one of the two-leggers – a short one. I think it's probably their puppy. It looks quite friendly, though it's hard to tell with creatures that don't have a tail to wag. I give it a floppy greeting with mine. The short two-legger squats down in front of me and peers into my face. It strokes my head with its front paw and makes soothing noises that sound something like,

"It's OK Bouncer, they'll be back soon. We're going to look after you for a while. Don't worry about the ornaments – I break stuff all the time."

There are only two sounds that I recognise there. One of them is 'Bouncer' – that's me. The other one is 'OK'. That's a word that means you can stop sitting or staying or whatever it was they told you to do and bounce about again. So I do. Unfortunately, I bump into the crouching two-legger and it falls over. Then I accidentally stand on it and it squeals. Oh no, have I broken this as well?

"Sorry, sorry, sorry," I whimper pathetically.

I give it some pink, wet kisses to show I didn't mean to flatten it. It waves its legs in the air and makes a funny noise. Is it hurt? Is it in distress? ... No, I think it's laughing. That's something that two-leggers do when you do something whacky, like chasing your tail or dragging the cover off your bed and running madly about with it. So I do both of those things and the short two-legger makes the noise again and gives me some more pats. I'm beginning to feel better now. I rush about some more and make squeaky noises. It doesn't sound *quite* like two-legger laughing, but pretty close.

Then the big two-leggers come to see what all the fuss is about. They are obviously not pleased to see their puppy squirming about on the floor and my blanket trailing fluff and dog hair all over their nice clean kitchen. They make their puppy leave me alone until I've *'settled in'*, whatever that means.

—

I'm depressed again. I lie and wonder about things for a while. How am I supposed to do this 'settling in'? I don't know what it is or how to do it. We didn't cover 'settling in' at Puppy Training. Also, I'm lonely. I sit up, lift my head and give the universal 'I'm-here-where-are-you?' dog call:

"Ah-ooooooooooo! Ah-ooooooooooo!"

I hope the short two-legger will hear me and come back. Actually they *all* come back and tell me to shut up. The big ones mumble to each other grumpily. I can tell they are beginning to think I'm a bit of a nuisance already. This is not good. I shall have to do something about it.

I roll onto my back with my paws in the air and try to look as cute and appealing as I can. It usually works. Yes, it seems to be working now. One of the big two-leggers makes sympathetic noises.

"Poor pet! You can see he's really missing them can't you," she says, *"Maybe if we take him a nice, long* <u>*walk*</u> *it might distract him a bit."*

I'm sure you can guess which word I've picked up out of all that lot – it happens to be one of my favourites. *WALK*? Oh yes, any time you like – ready when you are. I do a quick flip-over, grabbing my ball-on-a-string as I turn and I'm at the back door in a flash. Now they are all making the laughing noise. They're putting on their wellies; they've got my lead and some poo-bags. This is more like it. Maybe I'll be OK here after all ... for a while anyway.

—

Sea of Love

by Fiona Atchison

Diving in the depths of seething love –
we plunged!
foregoing the foreplay of a temperate toe dip
Immersing our limbs in rivulets of desire, we
basked, besotted in a steam of self-indulgence.

Perilous waves of passion swept sense away,
time trickled through Sandman fingers and,
drowning in a whirlpool of lust we sank,
anchored tightly, one heart to the other.

But emotions – fickle and slippery as eels,
flip around in lovers' turbulent minds
Influenced by the ebb and flow of moods,
we squirmed, recoiling from each touch.

As the tempest's course veered inward,
our anchors came as crushing millstones
How detestable those squally days,
which shipwrecked our wayward love.

A Relative Surprise

by Helena Sheridan

"He thinks you are a very nice young woman," Pippa's aunt announced.

Pippa shook her head, then continued to tug at the straggly weeds that threatened to choke the herbaceous border. She knew it would only be a matter of time before Aunt Elsie, the perpetual matchmaker, would try to generate her interest in someone else. This time, it was to be David Parks, the middle aged bachelor who lived four doors down. How she rued her decision to spend the summer in the Highlands with the elderly widow.

There was no denying that, although shy, David was reliable and had become quite a fixture around the place, offering to help with the most trivial things. Pippa recognised the ploy to draw them together and made sure that, on those days, she had 'something else to do in town'.

"He never married you know," Aunt Elsie prompted from her shaded sun lounge. "His fiancée died in a car crash." After a moment of respectful silence, she leapt back into action. "So ... he's quite unattached."

Pippa slammed down her trowel.

"Really? So?" There was a tinge of warning in her voice.

Aunt Elsie glanced pathetically towards her late husband's garden.

"I'm just saying, it doesn't do to go through life alone. So I've invited David round for dinner on Saturday."

"What?" Pippa objected at the blatant conspiracy.

Aunt Elsie remained unruffled. "I thought it would be an opportunity for the two of you to get to know each other better."

Pippa sighed. The thought of a tedious evening with the socially awkward David seemed too much to bear.

"But auntie ... David's ... well," she searched for the perfect excuse, "let's face it, there's a bit of an age difference."

"What has age to do with it?" Aunt Elsie protested. "It means nothing these days."

Pippa stared at the defensive woman and shrugged in defeat. Clearly her aunt had put a lot of effort into planning this meeting, and would refuse to be dissuaded. There was only one thing for it; she would have to be equally cunning!

She was glad when Saturday finally arrived and she was able to put her counter-plan into action. Clicking her bedroom door quietly behind her, Pippa drew the sleek, black cocktail dress from the shopping bag.

"Perfect," she giggled.

She pulled the dress over her head, checking her reflection in the long bedroom mirror. The soft material flattered her well-rounded figure. Freeing her hair from the constricting band, she allowed her chestnut curls to tumble provocatively over her shoulders. The transformation was already astounding.

"Better hurry," Aunt Elsie called through the door, "David will be here any minute, and you'll have to entertain him while I prepare the dinner..."

Pippa glanced in amusement at her face in the mirror. Several applications of stodgy, brick tinted make-up had completely covered her normally fresh complexion. She pouted her well-glossed lips into a scarlet bow. She could just hear Aunt Elsie welcoming David at the door.

"Pippa will be right down. It will give you a chance to ... speak to her."

Pippa swept downstairs.

"David, how are you?" she made a theatrical entrance into the room. "I've been longing to get to know you ... better," she purred.

David perched uneasily on the sofa, his wiry, ginger hair and perplexed expression giving him the appearance of a distraught terrier.

"There's something I ... must ask you," he muttered.

Pippa inched nearer.

"Perhaps you've noticed I've been coming around quite a bit?" His voice shook.

"Yes." She ran her hand along the back of the sofa towards him.

"Well," he swallowed hard, "your aunt thought I should ask you ... I know she thinks the world of you and ... I know there's an age difference..."

"Age doesn't matter when you're in love," she confirmed her aunt's opinion, placing her arm round his shoulder.

With renewed strength David peeled her away.

"Great! Then your aunt and I can get married as soon as possible!"

Pitlochry: a perfect paradigm

by Catherine Lang

The theatre, the reservoir,
fat ducks on Cuilc pond.
A row boat on Loch Faskally,
a dearth of sea and sand.

A sanctuary in childhood
far from wartime fears.
Progenitor of memories
augmented down the years.

A trek up to the Soldier's Leap
while salmon sclim the steps,
to seek their own posterity
in Tummel's gravelly depths.

Uisge beatha at Edradour
or tea on swards of green,
where the Lady of the Loch
drinks in the tranquil scene.

Nestling in the towering trees,
the Coronation Bridge
bears speeding travellers, north or south,
unheeding, unenriched.

—

A Quiet Night In

by Greta Yorke

Helen burst through the front doorway and clattered down the plastic box which groaned with forward planning, dairy, 30 Maths jotters and 30 Writing jotters, still to be marked. She had survived another week at Northfield Primary and Friday night brought a feeling of euphoria. It meant takeaway and definitely no school work.

"Friday night I love you," she shouted as she collapsed into the pine carver in the kitchen. Husband Ross was going out; he was meeting up with a friend who was home on holiday from Australia. Add to this the fact that *Falling in Love* with Meryl Streep and Robert De Niro, one of her all-time favourites, was on Film4, it was all looking good, very good.

As she passed the lounge she caught twins, Claire and Laura, sprawling over the sofas.

"We're going clubbing tonight, Mum. The girls are coming over about eight. We'll get ready here."

Claire's words were received, then lost in what they actually meant – Vikki and Kerry, outrageous fun, blaring music and laughter that escalated after one or two vodkas slid down amid the preening and makeup. Helen stoically decided this would not interfere with her plans. Ross was picking up the takeaway on his way home. After dinner she'd have plenty time to soak and relax before the girlie mayhem crescendoed.

She struggled out of jacket, scarf and boots and eased into her slippers. How welcoming they were. Now she was home.

Rather than disturb her clearly exhausted offspring, Helen filled the water jug and set three places at the kitchen table. Ross arrived with the food then, with a grunt of acknowledgement, he thundered up the stairs. Helen arranged the curries and rice on warm plates, tore the Naans and put them in the bread basket.

"Dinner's ready girls!" she called and surprisingly their appearance was almost instant. Helen poured water into their glasses and the three quickly settled in and attacked` the meal.

Both girls were halfway through degree courses at the nearby university and they usually came home with interesting gossip, which was kept for Friday night debrief. It reminded Helen of her own escapades while studying. Some of these were shared but others, too precious, remained treasured memories. The girls listened to Helen's staffroom tales with respectful forbearance, wondering why anyone would ever choose teaching as a career. Staff being kicked, spat upon and verbally abused was all too common, while endless assessment and reporting deflated everyone, especially the longer-serving members. Friday brought a euphoric rush with the end-of-day bell.

"Where's my new striped shirt? I'm going to be late! I've looked but it's not in the drawer," came from upstairs.

"Yes it is, you haven't looked properly," Helen rolled her eyes at the girls.

After a reasonable pause came,

—

"I've got it. It was right at the back, I didn't put it there! Have you seen my navy jumper?"

"It's in the airing cupboard, all nice and fresh for you," Helen replied shaking her head. "I blame the mothers!" she said to the girls. "If you have sons, don't pander to their helplessness."

"Don't worry," said Claire, "there's no fear of that!"

The girls returned to sofas and soaps. Helen tidied the kitchen, wondering where she'd gone wrong, then headed upstairs. Ross was slapping aftershave on his face as she passed the open bathroom on her way to their bedroom.

"Are you sure it's Dan you're meeting?" she teased but he clearly wasn't listening. He swept past her, grabbed his jumper, kissed her on the cheek and left.

"Won't be late, you might still be up," he called from the stairs, then Helen heard the front door close.

Helen gathered toiletries, bathrobe, towels and some magazines.

She undressed, stepped under the shower and washed the school away with the shampoo bubbles. Then, with body and hair wrapped in soft towelling, Helen tripped through to her bedroom to blow dry her hair. With the business side of it done she returned to the bathroom to light scented candles and drizzle a creamy fusion into the running water, wondering what dragon fruit and camu camu berries might look like. Helen turned off the water as the bubbles met the tap, dropped her towel and stepped in. She sat down, reached for a magazine, then lay back resting her head on the sumptuous bath pillow as fragrant froth covered her body with the promise to 'revive your senses and feel renewed'. This was indulgence.

Helen grinned as the rich lather covered her weary body, like snow rendering the most unsightly scene beautiful. She was vaguely aware of Vikki and Kerry's cackling arrival as she absorbed the gossip of celebs like Brad and Angelina, Gwyneth and Cameron. Too soon the bubbles were disappearing, leaving a meringue-like archipelago. She continued catching up on info with which she might impress the younger members of staff, but was quickly interrupted as her eyes began to itch. Helen tossed down the magazine and rubbed her eyelids gently at first, then more forcibly as the itch increased but this was clearly not working. She ran cold water on a facecloth and placed this on her closed lids.

This brought some relief and Helen again reclined, this time allowing thoughts of her university days to come to mind and of her first love, Mark. He had been two years ahead of her, studying Geography and Archaeology. Oh, those days! She smiled as she remembered one particular summer day when he'd borrowed his father's car and they'd driven to the coast and lain in each other's arms on the sand beneath the sunny eiderdown and, between kisses, planned their future. How she'd adored him. She could almost feel those gnawing pangs of first love. When Mark had graduated he'd gone abroad to work with the VSO. Frequent letters petered out; then Helen had met Ross. She wondered where Mark might be now. Was he happy? Did he ever think of her? She tried to imagine bumping into him. Would they recognise each other? Helen was just trying to

—

visualise how he might look now when she was jolted back to the present with an almighty bump bump thump, then shrieks of hysteria. She shot upright.

As the facecloth fell away it became apparent that her eyelids were so swollen they would barely separate. She peered through the slits, clambered out of the bath and threw on her bathrobe, groping her way to the door.

"What's happened?" she called from the doorway.

"Oh Mum," Claire shouted, "it's Kerry She's fallen downstairs. Geezo, Mum! What's happened to you?" she added as Helen appeared at the top of the stairs.

"I don't know what happened," cried a tearful Kerry. "I must have tripped, my ankle's really sore and I've bumped my head."

"Her ankle's huge already," Laura reported.

Helen could just make out a crumpled Kerry below and told the girls to keep comforting her while she fumbled into sweatshirt and joggers. This looked like a hospital job. Claire tried to phone her dad but he'd left his mobile on the hall table.

The girls helped Kerry into the back seat of the car, Vikki sitting between her and Helen, resting the injured ankle on Helen's lap. By now Helen looked as if she's done rounds with Mike Tyson.

"You'll both be sorted soon," Laura reassured as Claire drove her mother's car.

When they arrived at Accident and Emergency, Vikki fetched a wheelchair for Kerry while Laura guided her mum through the automatic doors. Vikki followed, pushing Kerry. Claire phoned Kerry's mum, then arrived from the car park as the two casualties were giving their details to the receptionist. Thankfully the department wasn't busy for a Friday night and they sat quietly waiting. There was only one other patient in the waiting room, a young lad holding a bloodied towel to his head. He was called almost immediately and left a trail of blood as he disappeared through automatic doors with a nurse. The gang was entertained by a cheery orderly who'd arrived to clean the floor. After about fifteen minutes the nurse returned for Helen and took her to the treatment room. Soothing liquid was drizzled over now bulging eyelids as Helen listened to the lilting Irish brogue of Dr O'Farrell. He assured her that the discomfort would soon ease. She'd had an allergic reaction to either the dragon fruit or camu camu berries. He prescribed drops which would soothe and reduce the swelling. The nurse put drops into the corners of both eyes and told Helen to return to the waiting room.

Meanwhile Kerry was now being examined by the young and very handsome Dr O'Farrell. The three girls hung on his every word, totally captivated. He examined Kerry's head first then, having decided that there was no concussion, he inspected her ankle which had now doubled in size. Poor Kerry winced but fought back tears as her friends comforted her. Then she was wheeled through to x-ray and the girls went to find Helen. Amazingly her eyes were much improved, just a little swollen and red. When the nurse returned she gave Helen her prescription and they waited for Kerry's return. Although the unfortunate Helen hadn't really seen Dr O'Farrell clearly, the girls

—

assured her he was 'really fit'. Well, she could always dream.

When Kerry eventually returned, her ankle was firmly strapped and supported by the wheelchair's footrest. The x-ray showed the ankle was not broken but badly sprained and poor Kerry looked quite grey. Her expression changed though when her mother swished through the automatic doors and rushed to cuddle her. Helen related the information given by the nurse and Kerry's mum thanked her, then wheeled her wilting daughter away.

"Take care, we'll call you tomorrow. Wasn't that doctor awesome?" Vikki shouted after them. Kerry waved a 'thumbs up' in response.

Claire dropped Vikki off at her house, then returned home.

"Well, so much for a night out," said Claire as she and Laura disappeared into their rooms leaving Helen to tidy the bathroom chaos. She changed into her cosy pyjamas; the film was about to start. Still hopeful of a little indulgence Helen busied herself heating milk for a truly expensive organic hot chocolate. She savoured its richness as she stirred the milk into the powder.

Helen curled up on a sofa and melted into its comfort, hugging her mug of chocolate heaven. She switched on the film to find Meryl Christmas shopping and just about to meet Robert. It's all Christmassy and snowy and New Yorky, and Helen was right there among it all.

Then Ross was gently stroking her cheek.

"Hey sleepy, sorry I'm late. You waited up for me, that's nice. We had a great night. Tom's hardly changed at all, just a bit of a twang," he went on. "I

99

hope you had your nice relaxing evening. You look like you've been out on the town," he grinned noting her watery, red eyes now open.

Helen peered past Ross to the blank screen. She'd fallen asleep and missed it all, the meeting, the falling in love, the angst, the lot.

"Oh, I've missed it," groaned Helen.

"Let's get upstairs, I'm exhausted!" said Ross oblivious to her disappointment. He wrapped his arm round her and they headed upstairs. "That must have been some film!"

Ross lifted back the quilt and gently eased Helen onto the bed. She sighed and lay down, rolled over and curled up. She wouldn't remember Ross placing the duvet over her or kissing her cheek. She had drifted to that secret place where the most dashing of heroes, some now with treacly Irish accents, could be found.

Cinderella Smith

by Fiona McFadzean

A bargain it was
that bolt of cloth,
bought from a gypsy
at the door.

The old treadle whirred,
producing curtains, table
cloth, cushion covers and,
Horror of Horrors,
a puffed sleeve dress for
my High School dance.
I wanted to die.

Decked in sky blue gingham
I fitted in at home, especially
in the kitchen.
Not so in the assembly hall.
Standing, kin to a sore thumb,
among the taffetas and satins
I wanted to hide.

Luckily the boy next door arrived
and claimed me as his partner;
each other's port in a storm we
were, comfortable together.
I was almost relaxed

when Tom gasped, "Wow! Look at her.
Oh yes, I must have some of that"
There stood Faye in layers of pink net,
looking to my mind like a spare loo roll doll.
I wanted to run.

Until Tom exclaimed, "Just the job for
keeping the blackbirds off the strawberries."
Then he smiled and pulled me close and...
I wanted to stay.

The LiterEight Writers

LiterEight is a group of eight female writers, all of whom live in Ayrshire on the south west coast of Scotland. Some of us were born there; others have made it their home for many years.

Like most writers, we have all been scribbling away for years while dealing with life challenges, families and careers. Each of us has her own favourite genre but over the years we have striven to hone our writing skills in many different fields.

Fiona Atchison has had an interesting and varied career including, working with horses; being a joint proprietor in a Wine Bar and Nightclub and teaching children with special needs. She currently works as an Occupational Therapist and writes part-time. Fiona has had poetry, and short stories published in magazines and anthologies. She also ventured into writing song lyrics which led to a collaboration with a musician, producing three CDs.

Her writing success at the Scottish Association of Writers includes a first for poetry in 2005, first for Science Fiction in 2008 and she won the General Novel Competition in 2014.

Maggie Bolton is English by birth but has lived in Scotland with her husband for the past twenty odd years (not all that odd). She taught both in the UK and in Germany and now retains contact with children as a Rainbow Guide Leader. No surprise then that her main interest is children's writing, but she also enjoys other writing forms, provided it's not too serious (Don't look for 'deep and meaningful' unless you have a lot of time to waste.) She is also a painter, exhibiting locally and would like to break into illustration.

Helena Sheridan was born in Biggleswade. Her family emigrated to Melbourne, Australia, returning to the UK in 1976 and she now lives in Scotland. Her keen interest in drama has resulted in her plays and comedy monologues being performed in various Scottish theatres. She has also written children's educational scripts for BBC Radio Ulster and is published in women's fiction, poetry and articles both in the UK and abroad.

Lesley Deschner enjoys writing short stories, articles, humorous poems, sketches and plays. Her passion for acting has introduced her to local Ayrshire theatre companies, such as Hipshot and Polymorph with whom she has taken roles. She stepped down from her the Council of the Scottish Association of Writers (March 2014) and her role as Secretary for the Writers' Summer School, Swanwick, Derbyshire (August 2014) to begin a 2-year Part-time PG Diploma in Counselling at Strathclyde University.

Janice Johnston has lived on the same Ayrshire farm for most of her life. She has written for a good chunk of that time, too, but only seriously from the mid-90s. She joined a local writers' club and began to have success with children's short stories and woman's magazine short stories. She has been published in magazines in Australia and South Africa, as well as the UK. For a number of years, she wrote scripts for education programmes for BBC radio. When not writing, she helps her husband on the farm and tries to keep track of her two grown up sons.

Catherine Lang started writing in her teens and her love of words led to a life-long career in public affairs. She wrote on myriad topics – briefing materials, speeches, feature articles – and her work regularly appeared in print and electronic media. For the past decade she has added book reviews, fiction, children's writing, poetry and drama to her portfolio and has enjoyed success both in publication and in competition, including winning the inaugural May Marshall Book Review Trophy at the Scottish Association of Writers' Conference in 2007, and again in 2013.

Fiona McFadzean was hooked on writing after winning a National Competition in primary school, enjoying drama and poetry in particular. For many years she wrote sketches, revues and plays for amateur dramatics and youth theatre. She has also devised training programmes for Adult Literacy and modified GCSE coursework for students with Special Educational Needs while working in Education. She has also taught creative writing to adults and teenagers and she still teaches Sunday School where she uses storytelling and drama to get the message across to Primary 1 and 2. After serving on various writing committees, Fiona decided that it was time to concentrate on her personal output and, at present, is working on both a crime and a romantic novel.

Greta Yorke is a retired primary teacher who lives in west Scotland. Story writing started at school where she transformed jotters into storybooks, but she did not begin writing seriously until 2008 when she joined Ayr Writers' Club. Since then she has enjoyed success when her children's story won first place in the Scottish Association of Writers' Competition in 2010. She has had poetry and articles published, in addition to children's stories online.

To learn more about the LiterEight writers and their two earlier collections, *A Literary Confection* and *Dark Twists*, visit www.litereight.co.uk

Notes